MW01126912

The Road Back to
THUNDER HAWK

George Gilland
and
Sharon Daggett Rasmussen

Copyright © George Gilland and Sharon Daggett Rasmussen
All rights reserved.
ISBN-13: 9781542341684
ISBN-10: 154234168X
Library of Congress Control Number: 2017904933
CreateSpace Independent Publishing Platform
North Charleston, South Carolina

Book Two of the Red Eagle Series

This book is the second volume in a series by the writing team of George Gilland and Sharon Rasmussen that tells the story of Robert Gilland, also known as Red Eagle or *Wanbli Luta*, who tries to make a life in the new twentieth century on the Standing Rock Sioux Reservation in South Dakota.

For Damen, Sheri, Kirsten, and Madison

Preface

The Road Back to Thunder Hawk is the second book in a series that tells the story of Robert Gilland, also known as Red Eagle or *Wanbli Luta*, who tries to make a life in the new twentieth century on the Standing Rock Sioux Reservation. Like many on the Dakota frontier, he was a half-breed with a white father and Lakota mother. The Buffalo Nation, *Tatunkan Oyatewas*, of his Lakota ancestors had been reshaped into the Great Sioux Reservation, which had become a new frontier for white pioneers. By breaking up the reservation into homesteads, the government encouraged these new immigrants to settle among the Indians in the hope that the natives would learn "civilized ways" from the whites, who were in large welcomed by the Lakota.

Robert's father, Benjamin Gilland, arrived in what was Dakota Territory in 1875, joined the army, and served at Fort Lincoln under General Custer. Sergeant Gilland had remained behind at Fort Lincoln in charge of the stable on the day that the general made his famous last ride. In 1881 he married Elizabeth McEldery, who had been raised by her mother Elizabeth Bob Tail Bull and her stepfather Samuel McEldery. As the Sioux were considered to be enemies of the US government while the Indian wars were still in progress, Benjamin had to resign from the army in order to marry Elizabeth.

Along the Trail to Thunder Hawk included many of the stories that Robert relayed to his family and friends. This volume continues the story of his adventures during the turbulent years of World War I and Prohibition. Robert joins other Lakota soldiers using their native language in the trenches to help defeat the Germans. After the war, he wants to return to ranching, but times are tough and cattle prices low, so along with his sister's husband, Tubby, and his hidden still, he looks to other sources of income ushered in by Prohibition.

Acknowledgments

We have tried to tell this story in Robert Gilland's voice as much as possible. We want to thank all the friends who helped piece together the facts along the way, especially Beth Summers Ebert. Robert Gilland and Slim Summers served together throughout the Great War, and Beth generously shared her mother's letters written by Slim from the war zone.

We would like to thank the many friends and family members who read the early drafts of our work and responded with enthusiasm and encouragement. We would especially like to thank Damen Gilland, Sheri Gilland, Kirsten Woodward-Allen, Amanda Dubin, Anne Wolmeldorf, Carol Zimmerman, Sherry Daggett, and Karen Clarkson.

George Gilland
e-CHA-h'dah Tatanka Owichakuya kah (Brings Back Buffalo)
February 2017

Sharon Daggett Rasmussen
Wakinyela Ska (White Dove)
February 2017

Contents

CHAPTER I

Leaving Home

I could see the glint of early-morning sunlight on the tracks as I searched the horizon for the coal smoke from the Milwaukee Railroad's engine. Once again I was standing around the station with my family looking down the tracks waiting for a train. This time it would take me off to fight a war half the world away from Thunder Hawk.

"Ever since President Wilson declared war on Germany, you've been itching to join up," said my older brother, Ben. "Now you are going off to see if it's worth fighting for a country that won't even let you vote."

"I'm not the only one from around here," I said. "I heard that Felix Fly and Snooky Goodreau signed up too. They were both at that Fort Yates boarding school with us. Maybe they wanted a chance to 'count coup' on Kaiser Bill. They don't put Indians into separate Indian units like they put colored soldiers—I guess since Custer had got his just deserts, most in the army figured it was better to have us on the same side in fighting a war.

"And right now, army pay of a dollar a day looks better than standing around for commodity rations at Fort Yates. If I'm careful and don't spend all that army pay on high livin', I can get back to being a rancher again.

"I'm sorry you aren't going too, but somebody has to keep Abe out of trouble," I said knowing that was the last thing Ben would do for him.

Ben seemed to be thinking on things a bit more than usual that morning. "Half-breeds like us have one foot in the ways of the white world and one in the Lakota ways. As far as Uncle Sam is concerned, we are Indians, and a lot of white settlers here in South Dakota still worry about the Lakota looking for another Custer fight. Some people back east think that mixing with white soldiers will be a civilizin' influence. When Indians make war, they are savages, but when whites do, it's civilizin'."

I couldn't argue with him, and I didn't want to on that day, so I said, "I guess eight years of boarding school and seven years of busting rocks in prison prepared me some for the army. In both places, we had to wear uniforms and get up, go to bed, stand up, and sit down when we were told. Though I don't think that the army will wash our mouths out with green soap for talking Lakota like those nuns did at boarding school."

"Just remember all you learned from your big brother and come back home safe so we can raise at least a little more hell before we're too old," replied Ben as the train rolled in.

My younger brothers, Abe and Jimmy, were near grown now, but young enough that Mother hoped they wouldn't be going off to join the army.

"I'll be here with a good horse broke for you when you get back," Abe said in his loudest voice and then added more softly, "Don't forget to come back."

Jimmy said, "Remember who will be doing all the work around here while you're gone." And he gripped my hand like the strong young man he had become.

Bessie was wearing her best summer dress and a ribbon to keep her short, dark hair from bouncing around too much in the wind. Her husband, Charlie Fero, stood by her on the platform wearing his Sunday "cowboy" outfit, complete with chaps and red leather wrist gauntlets. Charlie was a farmer, but like a lot of farmers, he'd rather be seen as a rancher. "Don't be taken in by those French girls.

I know you won't do anything foolish," Bessie said with a weak little smile that didn't hide the tear running down her cheek.

"Don't take any guff, and come back when you've knocked some sense into those Krauts," said Charlie.

My whole family was there but not my friend Brave Bear. As boys we had spent so many summers together with our *Unci*, my great aunt *Wakinyela Ska*, down on the Grand River, as she taught us Lakota ways. But Brave Bear had not learned how to tread carefully in both the white and Lakota worlds. I thought for a moment how much he would have liked being a soldier in this big war, but by now his bullet-riddled bones had been picked clean by crows and eagles and his spirit long departed.

"I lost a lot of my young years waiting for the wheels of white justice to turn around. But I can still ride and shoot better than most, and probably the army wants me to carry a gun," I said as I spotted this long drink of water feller trotting up.

"I figured I'd better go along to the army with you, keep you out of trouble," he said as he swept himself up onto the caboose platform.

"I wondered if you had changed your mind. Guess folks from Missouri are used to being a day late," I replied. Turns out I signed up for the army at the same time as a tall, skinny fellow who went by the name of Slim Summers, who had been doing some work for my dad. Slim had come west from Missouri and was looking for a little more excitement than training mules offered, so he had gone up to Lemmon to talk to the army recruiters.

Slim didn't want to show that he was a little nervous waiting for that train, so he started in asking me a lot of questions about Dad, Mother, the ranch, and other sorts of things. For openers, he asked where Dad had come from. I explained, "Dad had come west for adventure when he was young," but mostly he had headed out just ahead of the law. He didn't exactly leave his home in Muncie, Indiana, voluntarily. He was dancing with a pretty gal, and her boyfriend got jealous and called him outside. Dad punched the fellow once and took the fight right out of him, but when he hadn't come to next day, there was talk of charging Dad with murder if he should die."

"Well, that don't surprise me," Slim replied, "I seen how strong his arms and shoulders are, even for a man his age."

"That's because he worked in his family's blacksmith shop since he was little. Anyway, before the sun rose, he slipped down to the railroad yard and hopped in a boxcar on a train heading west. He didn't know where it was going, but the end of the line was at Bismarck in Dakota Territory. He joined up with the army there and served for a few years in the Seventeenth Infantry under Custer at Fort Lincoln," I explained.

"You mean General Custer? The one who got wiped out at the Little Big Horn River in '76?"

"Yeah, but he didn't think too much of the general. He thought he was an ornery cuss and a big bag of wind. Later on, Dad was stationed at Fort Yates, and that's where he met my mother."

"What was your mother doing at the fort?" he wanted to know.

"Mother's stepfather, Samuel McEldery, was a fur trader who had set up a trading operation near the fort. Mother's people were Hunkpapa Lakota and Yankton-a, who had pretty much always camped along the Grand River. Mother was called Red Bird (*Zintkala Luta*) by her mother's Lakota family and Elizabeth by the whites at the fort. She and her sisters all spoke English as well as Lakota and knew something of the ways of both the Lakota and whites," I went on telling him.

"When she and Dad decided to get married, he had to muster out of the army. In 1881, you couldn't be married to the enemy and stay in the army, and in those days the US government still regarded the Sioux as the enemy," I related.

He went on quizzing me. "The Gilland ranch is a pretty nice spread. Most people here don't have such good land, or so much of it. How did your family end up with the best land around?"

"Dad took on the job of hunting game to feed the railroad crew that was building the rail line from Mobridge on the Missouri River on west across the reservation. He had covered a lot of ground on horseback and knew that the land where Chief Thunder Hawk had his winter camp was some of the best. When the Standing Rock Reservation land was allotted to Indians and then to whites for homesteading, he and Mother settled on a claim along the Grand

River. With a bunch of kids, each entitled to a quarter section, the Gilland ranch started off as a fair-sized operation.

"Our house and some of the other ranch buildings were taken from Fort Yates when they closed the garrison. Dad and some of his army friends dismantled officer's houses, hauled them over the frozen river in the winter to the Thunder Hawk area, and reconstructed them on their homesteads for their mixed-blood families. Of course, Thunder Hawk wasn't a town when the folks first settled there, but it has grown up into quite a bustling little community."

"You bet it is," threw in Charlie, joining the conversation. "We've got three churches, two taverns, a pool hall, a post office, two grain elevators, and of course the big new schoolhouse."

"So many things changed during the years I was away at school and college," said Bessie, a bit wistfully looking off to the east.

"And a lot changed while I was away," I said, not knowing just how much telling my story needed for Slim. But the train was still a long way off, and once headed down that road, I charged on. "Half a square mile of this land once was mine—the quarter section just east of the folks' homestead. Each of us kids got a quarter section. Ben and I were just starting out on our own in the ranching business when some things got out of control.

"A bunch of us boys from around Thunder Hawk were herding cattle from the Indian Agency at Fort Yates out to different ranches along the Grand River. A couple of the Duncan brothers showed up with some whiskey, and we got pretty drunk and got on the fight. My cousin Tom Powers was shot and killed. I shot at him, all right, but it was self-defense, and a lot of other guns were fired, too.

"The white jury in Aberdeen said I did it, and I got sent down to the federal penitentiary in Leavenworth, Kansas. I was down there busting rocks for seven years. Thanks to the warden, who was a decent sort, Mother and Dad, and Bessie's letter writing, I finally got a new trial and was set free." I stopped, thinking I'd said enough.

Bessie interjected, "I might have written the letters, but Dad signed them. The hardest part was just finding an honest lawyer," she said with a little stab of bitterness. "Now my favorite brother is leaving us again."

"I was somewhat more than glad to be home, but all my cattle and land are gone—sold off to pay those lawyers. There isn't much work for a ranchman without a ranch. So, Slim, now you know why I was so eager to join the army and take the government's dollar-a-day pay."

"I reckon you've paid your dues and then some, Bob. I'd heard some of what you told me around town, but it's better hearing it from you. Here's the train; let's get on with fighting Uncle Sam's new battles," he said, swinging his long legs up onto the caboose rail. "First stop on the way to Paris is Sioux Falls!"

Mother let a tear slide down her cheek, but mostly everyone was smiling. They kept waving their good-byes until we were out of sight. It would be a different trip this time.

I had only met Slim a few weeks earlier as I was riding into the homeplace from Ben Junior's homestead south of Thunder Hawk. When I got to the ranch that day, Dad had a team of mules out by the wagon and was trying to harness them, but every time he got close to them, one or the other would kick the collar right out of his hands. This tall kid was holding the mules' halter ropes, when Dad said to him, "Slim, you said you could drive a mule. Let's see how a mule skinner from Missouri gets a harness on those SOBs."

Slim stepped up in front of the first mule and whacked it hard alongside of its head. Then he grabbed the ear of the other one and twisted it down and said something to it. He gathered up the harness and walked right up behind the first mule, threw the harness on it, and did the same with the other one. He bridled them, snapped the reins to the bridles, picked up the reins, and drove them over to the tongue of the wagon. He backed them back to the doubletree, dropped the reins, went up front of the tongue to hook the neck yoke to the hame straps, and went back of it to hook the tugs to the singletrees. Then he picked up the lines again and hopped in the wagon and said, "Giddy up." And off they went!

Dad came walking over to me, sputtering, "I wouldn't believe it if I hadn't just seen it."

Slim came driving back in a little while and stopped right where he had started from. He jumped off the wagon and came right over with his hand out and said, "I'm John Summers from Chillicothe, Missouri."

Dad told him I was his son Bob, the one between Ben and Abe, and we shook hands. "It's about lunchtime," he said. "Let's go see what we can scare up for grub." Bess, my youngest sister, had married Charlie Fero—everybody called him Tubby even before he ate too much of Bessie's good cooking—and they had a place on Bess's quarter of land, a mile west of the folks'. Mother was over there, but I was sure she had left plenty of food to be found. When we got to the house, a drawing of a pot roast with an arrow pointing to the oven and a picture of a pie with an arrow pointing to the ice box was laying on the table. Mother couldn't write; she just never had a chance to go to a school. Anyway, Dad didn't have to look real hard to find plenty to eat.

After we had polished off the pie, Dad said, "Slim, you just as well take those mules down to the river and bring back a load of firewood. You can follow Bob; he knows the way." He turned to me and added, "Bob, you can go down to our winter camp and pick up a few calves and bring them up here—the boys missed about forty head of calves last fall when we gathered the herd. Ben has been catching them up and holding them there, but they're in his way now, and he wants to get them out of there so he can use the corrals for breaking horses."

I saddled a fresh horse and we were off. This horse was grain fed, and he really wanted to go, so I moved right along. After about ten miles, I figured I'd better slow down a little and let Slim and his mules catch up. When I looked back, hell, that Slim was right on my tail, and those mules weren't even working up a sweat yet.

I didn't tell Dad that even before I left from Ben's this morning, he had taken a buggy and was heading up to the Pretty Rock country just north of Thunder Hawk to pick up Maude Williamson. Maude had gotten pregnant last year. When Ben didn't act fast enough, she married Art Phillips, a man her father liked but nobody else did. They had had a fight, and Maude went home to her mother's. She had wrote Ben to come up, if he was still interested,

7

and to see his son. She would go home with him if he still wanted her. She had asked him to take her to a social at the Grand Valley Hall that night just a few miles east of our winter camp.

When we got to camp, I said to Slim, "Do you want to take in a pie social and dance at Grand Valley before we head out to basic training?"

"That's a pretty dumb question," he replied.

We got cleaned up and put on lots of tonic—we were standing tall and looking sharp. I was only about five feet eleven inches, but Slim was six feet two inches tall. He wouldn't ride a horse and wanted to take the mules to the dance hall in Grand Valley.

"Okay," I said, "I'll ride with you if you hitch them to the buggy, but I'm not riding to a social in that double box wagon!" The buggy it was, and we were off. I didn't quite know what to expect, but there were probably some people at the social who might not want to see me. A little lively dancing sure would be welcome after all the years gone. Grand Valley had changed some since I was last there with people living about everywhere, but the hall was the same. There was already a large gathering. I recognized some of the crowd, but there were a lot of new faces I didn't know. Ben and Maude were standing among the crowd, and they seemed happy to be together that night. I didn't see a baby with Maude; I figured that she must have left him with her mother. Abe and his new wife, Viola, were there too.

"There's Alma Pearson—her folks have a homestead south of Thunder Hawk. Isn't she about the prettiest gal you ever did see?" Slim asked, not expecting an answer.

There were several gals standing over where Slim pointed, so I wasn't sure which one was Alma, but I said, "Sure is. Are you going to introduce us, or just wave all night?" I tied up the buggy and went over to talk with Ben and Abe and got a big hug from both of their gals. Slim went right over to Alma and in half a minute was introducing her to all of us.

There was a clanging by the hall door, and a fellow was standing on a little platform. I thought he must be a politician, but he was holding a basket. "All you gents who are hungry gather around. We are selling this basket of food to the highest bidder.

Look how pretty it's decorated, and it's real heavy. There must be a lot good food inside. Buy it, and you get to go inside the hall and sit at a table and eat with the pretty gal who has prepared this lovely basket. Get your hands in the air. Who will give me five dollars?" The gals who prepared the baskets were waiting behind a curtain rigged up inside, hoping the right fella would buy theirs. Nobody was supposed to know beforehand whose basket it was.

I was going to bid, but Maude nudged me in the ribs and said, "That's Francine Warner's." I knew Francine from way back. She was a nice enough sort, but she worked outside all the time and usually wore men's clothes, including a dusty old felt hat. I doubted if she was much of a cook. I passed on bidding, but someone else bid, and sure enough, it was Francine's basket.

The baskets sold quickly. Slim had gotten Alma's, and I was beginning to think I wasn't going to get one when a pretty basket, decorated in pink, was held up. No one poked me, so I bid and got it. I was taken completely by surprise by who walked up to claim ownership of the basket—Lizzy Archambault. We were engaged to marry before I went to the pen, but that had ended abruptly when the jury in Aberdeen said that I murdered Tom Powers. She said then she didn't ever want to see me again. Now I was a free man and cleared of the charges, but I really had mixed emotions. Her dad had promised to shoot me if I ever came near his daughter. I had heard when I was in Leavenworth that she had married a dude from over Mobridge way. Most likely had a *cinca* (child) or two by now.

Viola must have seen the surprise on my face, and read my mind, because she said, "It'll be all right; you can eat with her but nothing more. She's still married, just up helping her folks. They are both in failing health, and she is just spending some time with them before the inevitable. Go on; it's a social!"

I knew the Archambault girls loved socials and always went to any in the area; still, I had reservations, and the old saying, "leave sleeping dogs lie," came to mind. But I walked up to claim my recent purchase.

"Hello, Liz," I said trying to keep my voice steady. She gave me a look that shot all the way through me, turned, and walked into the hall with the basket. I followed and as we were sitting down at a table, I said, "Thanks for not making a scene out front. I was about three-fourths expecting you to spit in my face and throw the basket at me."

"Oh, *Wanbli Luta* (Red Eagle)," she said, "I would never do that! I came tonight because Mother asked me to chaperone my baby sister, Phoebe. She's sixteen now and wanted to come with Pete Emmons, but Mother said she was too young to go alone with Pete. She could go if I went too, so here I am. I read in the papers about your new trial and knew you would be back in the area. I was sure hoping you would come to this social." She paused for a moment before saying, "I'm so sorry about the way things turned out. Dad was so bent on me not seeing you ever again that he made life at home pure hell, so I went to Mobridge and married the first guy who looked at me. That was the dumbest thing I've ever done. He's mean and drinks all the time—I never loved him, but now I despise him. Bob, you are the only man I will ever really love."

Then she said, "Dad made me write you and say I never wanted to see you again, but in my heart I knew it was the wrong thing to do. I know you wrote several times, but Dad always picked up the mail, and as soon as he got home, he would throw your letters in the stove. I never got to read any of them." Liz always did have a way of catching me off guard; maybe that's what I loved about her. But this really dumbfounded me. I wasn't sure what to say, so I didn't say anything and just started eating. But I sure was thinking hard.

I was still pondering the situation when some gent hollered, "Let's clear these tables out of here. We are going to have a dance." There were already three guys standing in a corner with a fiddle, guitar, and an accordion. Then the fellow who had hollered, asked, "Anyone here know how to call a square dance?"

No one volunteered, so finally I said, "I can call a couple, but I might be a little rusty at it."

"Great," he said. "We have a caller. Come on, couples; we will do two squares, four couples to a square."

I walked up to the gents in the corner and asked if they could play "Turkey in the Straw" and "Yellow Rose of Texas." They nodded and started playing, and the dance began. After the square dancing, the ladies were gathered up in a circle around the dance floor and gents in a circle around them; then the band started playing, and the ladies went right, and the gents went left. When the music stopped, you had to dance with the person you were facing. I somehow just happened to be facing Liz when the music stopped, so we had to dance together.

We were about halfway around the floor when a fellow I hadn't seen before gave me a shove from the side and said, "Get the hell out of here. We don't need your kind dancing with any of our women." This took me by surprise, but I knew what it meant. I sure didn't want trouble, but you can't run from it either. So I came around to square off at him, but a big frame was already in front of me. Slim gave that guy one punch, and he went sprawling back to the wall and slid down that wall like a wet rag. He slumped on the floor, knocked out colder than a cucumber. The music started playing again, so we all started dancing again, except for the guy who was knocked out.

When the music stopped, Liz took me by the arm and said, "Let's go for a walk." Outside we went. We walked down the trail quite a ways without saying a word; then Liz said, "*Mita wowastelaka* (My love), *Miye wacin kaga wowastelaka elta nis wana* (I want to make love to you now). This will be my last farewell to you because I have a feeling we'll never see each other again."

I said, "You surely will see me again. I'll be back from that little skirmish before you know it. This time I'll write you and send some money so you can get a place of your own till I get back. When I get out of the army, we can start fresh, and no one will ever come between us again."

"That sounds so wonderful," Liz said. "Call it a woman's intuition or a sixth sense, or plain foolishness, but I feel this will be our last night together, ever." When we got back to the dance, it was about over, and some people were already leaving. Liz gave me a hug and a little kiss on the cheek and scurried off to go home with Pete and Phoebe.

Slim wanted to take Alma home, but I didn't want to drive those mules, so I hopped in the back of Ben's buggy. He was heading for his homestead anyway and would go right by our camp.

I woke up to the sound of Slim sawing logs in the bunk across the room, so I got up and went out and started sawing up some logs, too. Slim could get loaded up when he woke up, and I could get to trailing calves to Thunder Hawk. We made it to the folks' place before dark and in time for supper. After we ate, Slim put the mules in the barn and told Dad, "Ben, those mules are well broke. You just have to show them who is boss; then they'll work fine for you!"

Then he hoofed it back to his brother Zachery's place a couple of miles to the east of Thunder Hawk.

CHAPTER 2

In the Army Now

The train headed for Sioux Falls had been rolling along for a while, when Slim, who was sawing logs, woke up with a stir and said, "Is there a privy on this train? I have to leak so bad my teeth are floating!"

"There is one at the back of the car," I answered, "but you can't flush it if we are in any city limits because it just drops down between the tracks, and town folks don't want that smell in their town!" I had learned that last month when I had come home by train from Kansas.

When we finally steamed into Sioux Falls, it was already about midmorning. We had to switch to a different train there, but someone was supposed to meet us, see we got fed, and get us on the right train for Kansas City, Missouri.

"All you sod hoppers, cowboys, Indians, and sheep herders who signed up for the army, fall in line in front of me," bellowed a big fellow dressed in a soldier's uniform standing in front of the train station. "You have two hours to shave, shower, eat, and be on the next train, so move it!" he added even louder. It was more like a cluster than a line, but sixty or so guys gathered in front of him, and he headed down the street. He took us to a gym first and said, "You guys get shaved and showered. There are ten showers, so some shave

13

first and some shower first, and I don't care who does what first, but get it done. I'll be back in fifteen minutes to take you to the mess hall. Anyone who isn't showered and shaved when I get back goes into the shower with his clothes on, and five of you other bastards will have to go in with him and scrub him down." He was back right on time, and every last one of us had shaved and showered.

Next we all followed him to a place he called the mess hall. As we went in, we grabbed a plate and walked along in a line. There were servers, just plopping food on every plate as we walked along. Everyone got the same amount of food, and you got what they served, even if you didn't want it. We ate fast sitting at tables and chairs set out in long rows. Water was on the tables, so who could ask for anything more! The food was pretty plain, but we were all hungry; so there wasn't any complaining, and we didn't even have to pay for it. The bellower soon had us fast-stepping it back to the train station and checked each guy's papers as we boarded the train for Kansas City. We were boarded on the last car ahead of the caboose—the regular people (civilians) were boarded in the cars ahead of us.

"Looks like another long, boring ride," I said to Slim, as we were plunking it down in a couple of seats, "and these seats are dang poor beds, but we'll soon be sleeping in army beds." Daylight was just breaking out, and we had been going and stopping all night. The train always slowed way down going up over hills and speeded up on the downhill sides. We were supposed to be in Kansas City by midmorning, so I figured we must be within a hundred miles or so from that big town. We had just started heading up a long hill, and I could feel the train slowing down, when I noticed three riders charging past our car and grabbing onto the car up ahead. I thought, "Them boys are sure anxious to get a train ride, or maybe we have some would-be train robbers." And the latter was what I decided was most likely. I nudged Slim and asked, "You got any extra money that you want to give away?"

"Certainly not," he said, "but if you're flat broke, I'll loan you a few bucks till payday."

"I've got enough to get by, but in about a minute, there very likely will be three boys coming through that door with pistols drawn and demanding our money. So if you want to keep your money, better get on one side of that door, and I'll get on the other side, and we will turn the situation around."

Slim was up and alongside of the door, faster than a cat. I was right behind and stood on the other side of the door.

I whispered, "I'll grab the pistol from the first one, and you take care of the second one. I'll put a pistol muzzle in the face of the third and back him up and shoo him off the train."

It wasn't a long wait. We soon heard someone coming at a fast pace. I managed to grab the first one's pistol and jerk it right out of his hand. It was in mine, and I was facing him. I motioned for him to step on in, and he did. As the second one's arm became visible, Slim whacked it so hard his pistol went bouncing off the floor. Slim didn't waste much time at picking up that pistol, and that kid, too, walked down the aisle raising his hands. The third lad didn't come waltzing in like the other two, but I could see his pistol, and it was coming up and was aimed at Slim. Slim had his back to the door now and was holding the attention of the other two. I aimed at the barrel of that pistol in the hand of the lad standing on coupling between the cars, and, by grab, it just wasn't there anymore. I quick-stepped out on the coupling. The lad out there had his back to me and was rubbing his hand. It must have stung a little when his pistol went flying. I grabbed him by the back of the collar and gave him a boot in the pants, and he did a high dive for the ditch.

Slim asked, "Now what? Should we hold them for the law or just shoot them?"

"Oh," I said, "let's give them a sporting chance. They can either sit and wait for the law to take them away when we get to Kansas City or get off this train within the next ten seconds." But I thought, "It will be a cold day in hell when I hold someone for the law." They took my second option and were sailing off that train in less than two seconds. I threw the pistol I had in my hand at the ditch, and Slim gave his a fling.

We were just getting back in our seats when the conductor came runnin' in, and said, "Three masked men just robbed all the people up front. Did they rob everyone in this car too?"

Slim replied, "No, they didn't take our money. Three guys did jump off the train ways back, though—they probably knew we didn't have any spare money."

The conductor just said, "Good, good," and left in a hurry.

Slim got to wondering if those boys were the Younger Brothers, "Them boys have a gang, and they have quite a reputation for robbing trains in Missouri."

"I don't know who they are, but I bet they will remember this little train robbery for a while," I said.

At last, the train was coming to a stop in Waco, Texas. I was a-thinking, "It'll sure seem good to get on solid ground again," when Slim said, "Let's go be soldiers!"

We stepped off the train, and right away we saw a fellow standing in front of the station wearing a soldier's uniform, so we headed his way. He pointed us toward a row of Model T trucks lined up to haul all of us new recruits to Fort Sam Houston. We were soon on our way. It didn't take long before we were getting acquainted with army chow and army bunks. We had it pretty easy the first couple of days, getting clothes and shots. Recruits like us had to have a shot for about everything they had a vaccine for so we could go to Europe. Then the fun began. It was up at 4:30 a.m., run two miles, back to the mess hall for chow, and then the training started. We were always in a hurry; then usually we would wait, but we fast shaped up good enough to pack a rifle, and we were ready to go fight the war.

I had said I wanted to be in the infantry, but the sergeant said, "You're on the list to be a medic. You can still shoot if someone is shooting at you, and you aren't treating the wounded."

I thought what a deal, but no use saying anything—it wouldn't do any good and probably just get me some extra duty. So I said, "Yes, sir," and thought, "I suppose someone has to take care of the wounded. Now I will be a *waken wicasa* (medicine man)." Slim was on the medic list too, so we did a quick course on how to treat the wounded. We had to go over to the hospital and work with the doctors there as they treated patients. Mostly we learned how to empty bedpans, but we did learn how to put on tourniquets and treat simple wounds. And we got a quick course in driving an ambulance. Mostly that meant driving fast and trying to dodge shell craters and potholes. The doctors kept telling us that we'd need to know this when we got in combat. In about three weeks of medic training, we were considered trained and ready to send across the big pond.

Another long train ride and then we were sitting on our duffel bags on the dock in New York Harbor, waiting to board a ship bound for France. Slim was writing a letter to someone, and I was sure thinking of Lizzy and South Dakota. I thought, *"Wagla wacin* (I want to go home)." I'd written her several letters—I sent them in care of Pete Emmons, and he made sure Lizzy got them—and this time she answered back. Slim seemed to always be writing to a certain Alma every time he had any spare time. I was kinda thinking they might have done something intimate when Slim took her home from the social at Grand Valley. Even though it's none of my business, I might tease Slim a little anyway. "Slim," I said, "looks like we are about to get a boat ride; you can finish your letter on the boat. After we get aboard, that gal will probably forget you before we get to France, anyway!"

They were starting to board troops, so we grabbed our bags and got in line. When we got below deck and were laying on our bunks, I grasped how big this ship really was—more like a train than a boat. It wasn't long before we were moving. I thought that we would get a lot of rest with nothing to do on this ship. I found that thought to be a real understatement. Our rest soon ended when a loud voice came out of a box hanging in the hall, "All medics report to sick bay!"

There were quite a few soldiers getting seasick and heaving all over. What a mess. I don't know if it was all that time on the train or a growing up on horseback, but neither Slim nor I got seasick. Us medics had to try to nurture the sick, and that was a job in itself. There wasn't much we could do for seasickness—just let it run its course. But having a medic look at them seemed to help some of the sick soldiers, and talking helped get their minds off their condition, so we spent a lot of time walking around looking at bed charts and talking.

I noticed the name on one bed chart was Earl Williamson, so I asked, "Are you related to those Williamsons in Pretty Rock country, north of Thunder Hawk, South Dakota?"

"Yes I am," he said. "That's where I come from."

"Private Robert Gilland," I replied, adding, "My dad is Benjamin Gilland."

"Maude is my oldest sister, and I know Ben Gilland Junior. He goes with Maude some, and he has been around a lot." Then he said, "I bet you are one of Ben's brothers; you look a lot like him!"

"Right you are," I said.

"Small world. We must have been back at Fort Sam together and didn't even know it. You know, that Ben is quite a guy. My folks have fifteen of us kids, and I'm the oldest boy, so we are always strapped for money, barely enough for food, but that Ben is always bringing something extra along, candy for the younger ones, sometimes some clothes. One time he had me go with him in the wagon, and we butchered a steer over on Cedar Creek. I hope he marries Maude someday. He'd sure be a swell brother-in-law!"

"From what I could tell the last time I seen Ben and Maude," I said, "it looked to me like it would only be a matter of time before they get hitched." I saw Earl several times after that, and we always found something to talk about.

In making my rounds in sick bay, I got acquainted with quite a few, but there were a couple of boys from back on the reservation I knew without an introduction. I was walking by one bed, and laying there was Harry Fast Horse (*Sunkawakan Luzahan*). We had been to Indian school together and helped at several horse roundups back at Standing Rock.

"*Mitakola waste* (Good day, my friend)," I said, which brought Harry sitting up in a heartbeat!

"*Waste, lila waste* (Good day, very good day), *Wanbli Luta* (Red Eagle). *Ake iyuskinyan wancinyankelo* (I'm glad to see you again), *Omapisni yelo* (I don't feel good)," he said looking a little on the green side.

I shook his hand and said, "You're far from being alone at being sick. About half the guys on this ship are in the same condition."

"Ran across Felix Fly yet?" Harry asked. "He came in yesterday. I think they put him down toward the other end of the bay somewhere."

"No, haven't seen him yet," I said, "but I'll get on down that way and see if he still knows me."

"Hey! *Wanbli Luta* (Red Eagle)." It was Snooky Goodreau, sitting on the edge of a bed about twenty feet down the row. He said, "I heard you guys talking Lakota. Don't you know by now that this army doesn't like us talking Sioux? They think we might be plotting an uprising or something." Then he laughed and walked a little unsteady over and shook my hand.

I said, "And don't you know, I'm a medic. My job is to keep all you sick sandbaggers in bed."

"I don't know what that is, but I'm not one of them, anyway," Harry replied.

Snooky asked, *"Tokiyatanhan yahi hwo?* (Where have you come from?)"

"Fort Sam Houston," I said, "and I suppose you were there too."

"Me and Snooky were at Fort Sam. We're in the signal company. We have it easy—all we have to do is sit in the main office and talk on a telephone to the boys at the front. If someone gets hurt, they call us, and we send *Wanbli Luta* up to the front line to patch 'em up and bring 'em back," said Harry.

Snooky said, "Felix is in the infantry, so he has to do all the shooting, but maybe we'll all get to go to the pool hall at nights and have a party!"

"You got it all figured out. Sounds good," I said, but I had a feeling that it just might be a little different than that. "What if, when we get to France, the French people don't speak Lakota or English, then what? And what if there are no pool halls?"

Snooky laughed. "Well, then we can just party with all the pretty women all night and be soldiers in the daytime." And he laughed again.

"We will be finding out what France is like very shortly," I said. "We should be landing there in a few days. In the meantime, I'd best be getting along—I'm working you know, *Iyunka yo* (Go to bed)." Them boys brought back a lot of old memories of when we were kids on the reservation and were going to Indian school together. Harry was really a fast runner at school. He once outran a race horse. He had told Fat McLaughlin, from over Fort Yates way, that he could outrun his horse for fifty meters. People made bets and it was a big attraction, and Harry outran the horse easily the first fifty meters, but I think he may have gotten beat if they would have called it one hundred meters. Snooky was at Indian school too, and he had a couple of very pretty sisters.

My friend Brave Bear and me had stayed with the Goodreaus back a few years and had helped cut horses at a horse roundup. There were several hundred colts to brand and castrate, and we got a dollar a head for each one we cut—we made good money, but it was hard work. As soon as we got one cut, the boys (Snooky included) would have another one tied down and ready to be cut. It took three days, and at night we slept in some tepees the Goodreaus had set up just beyond the corals. We were supposed to sleep in the boys' tepee, but somehow Brave Bear got us into the wrong one, and we woke up in the tepee with Snooky's sisters. That was kind of a mess in the morning, with the girls waking up screaming, pretending they hadn't noticed we were there all night. Brave Bear and I had been through quite a few experiences; some were even good. I wish he were here now, but he got killed in a shootout with the law a few months back—just before I got home from the federal pen.

When I had gotten around the end of the bay, there was no Felix, so I headed along the other side. I was just checking a chart when all of a sudden a big hand was on my shoulder. I thought not again, as I turned around kinda fast. I'll probably have to hang one on this gent. But I didn't—it was Felix Fly! We shook hands and I said, "Aren't you supposed to be in bed?"

"I was but had to go to the john and was just coming back when I seen you," Felix answered.

"I thought you would be playing ball for the White Sox by now," I said. We had played ball together back home many times, and Felix was one of the best ball players I'd ever seen. I'd heard that he had been offered a chance to play with the Chicago White Sox.

"They wanted me to, but I decided I'd try being a soldier first," he said, smiling a little.

CHAPTER 3

Lakota Doughboys

I was lying on my bunk, when Slim came in and said, "Have a look out the porthole—there's land coming up ahead!" I looked, and sure enough, I could see rolling hills. I thought kind of like back home but with more trees on them. We had crossed the English Channel and were going to get off the ship at a place called Saint Nazaire in France. We stepped off the boat on June 19, 1917, glad to be on dry land, and boarded a train that would take us inland to meet up with the other American Expeditionary Forces.

The Russians had given up on the Eastern Front, so Kaiser Wilhelm had reinforced the Western Front with a lot more troops, thinking the Germans about had the French and English whipped—and they did. But the United States had gotten into the fight on April 6, 1917, and joined forces with France and England. More than 600,000 US soldiers were already on the Western Front. We were among the lot, and General John "Black Jack" Pershing was in command along with a French field marshal Ferdinand Foch.

After a few weeks of training in France, we were moving out and heading north. Each company had sent its Signal Corpsmen out ahead to lay telegraph and telephone lines. There had been a battalion over on the north side, but they were really hit hard, and that's how a few of the enemy got through, at us. We had wiped out all the Germans we met, so now it should be a safe trip to the front line. I wondered how Snooky liked the pool halls and pretty women in France now. I hadn't seen either yet! We had been zig-zagging through the terrain for two miles or so when all of a sudden, one of the soldiers up front yelled "medic." I hustled right up and found both of our corpsmen lying there shot in the head and beyond help.

Our platoon sergeant came rushing over sizing me up with a long sideways look. "Private Gilland, aren't you some kind of Indian? Can you talk Indian? *Real* Indian? The Krauts have broken our codes and will understand every word we say, so we have to try something else." I don't know how many Indians that sergeant had seen up close before that day, but he sure seemed to know about talking in Indian. "There're a lot Indians fighting in this war, but some sure don't know how to talk Indian and some do. What kind of Indian are you? The last one I asked, said he was an Omaha Indian from Nebraska, he was even an officer, but the Omaha on the other end said he was talking mumbo jumbo and thought he was crazy. One of the Signal Corps guys said he sounded like his grandmother back in Palermo, Italy!"

He picked up the field telephone set, handed it to me, and said, "Try reaching the corpsmen from the other companies, but don't talk in English."

"Well, there're different kinds of Indians and different ways of talking. My mother's people are Lakota. There was a bunch of Lakota from South Dakota like me on the boat coming over, and there were a couple of Cheyenne from Montana, but I didn't meet any Omahas."

I took the phone and cranked on it, then said, "*Catka* (Left Hand)." We called Felix that sometimes back home.

Right away, "*Wanbli Luta?* (Red Eagle?)" I heard loud and clear over the phone. "*Sunkawakan Luzahan?*"

"*Taku ca yacin hwo?* (What do you want?)"

"*Iha Ohinni* (Always laughs)."

Snooky answered back with "*Nunpa na ake nunpa kin topa kte lo* (Two and two are four)."

"*Tuktel* (Where)?"

"*Owotanla an nata opawinge wikcemna moccasins* (Straight ahead one thousand feet)," Snooky said.

Catka said, "*Tuweni leta* (Nobody here)."

Harry said, "*Ttuweni leta.*"

Another voice came on from the battalion that we were supposed to be connecting with, "*Ena un koyala* (Stay put). *Unkia yuha iye* (We have it). *Tanyan icanun yelo* (You did well)."

The battalion had pinpointed where we were from the phone contact and had moved some big howitzer guns up behind Snooky. We heard a barrage of rounds to our right; then I heard Snooky again, "*Waniyan Wakan!* (Holy Spirit). *Wanblake sakowin wasicu's ungnahela tehmunga wankal, helanl wikcemna inyanka napa* (I saw seven white men suddenly fly high, then ten ran away). *Ihankeya wakokpapi* (They were thoroughly scared). *Ihpeya maza wakens ihakab* (Leave guns behind)."

In just a few minutes, we had company—a whole line of German soldiers came running at us. The first German was waving a stick with a white rag tied to it. When he got within a couple hundred feet, he yelled, "*Ve Surendoor.*" All the soldiers behind him had their hands on their heads, so it looked like we had us a bunch of prisoners. The platoon leader was quick to get some of our boys out around them and search them for weapons, but they didn't find any. So he assigned a detail of our soldiers to march them on to the battalion commander, Major Horace Bates, and let him take charge of the prisoners. There was well over a hundred German soldiers. Them howitzer rounds must have landed right in the middle of the whole bunch. It sure took the fight out of those still living.

We were at the front now or part of it, and I was still a medic but was soon temporarily assigned to the Signal Corps, till a trained Indian talker was found to replace me. Most of the boys in the company got busy digging in. Slim and I didn't have to do pick and shovel duty, so we stayed in the rest area and even had time to write a letter home, but no mail yet.

Our outfit was always trying to advance. One platoon would go ahead fifty or a hundred feet and dig in, then the next until the whole battalion was advanced, then, do it again. The Germans had started putting up a lot of resistance, so instead of trying to advance with the whole battalion, a reconnaissance platoon was sent out ahead of the line, stringing wires as they went; so when they spotted the enemy strongholds, they could report their locations. Then the big guns and tanks would blast the Germans, and the line would advance and catch up to us. Slim was sent along as a medic, but I went with the signal crew and Felix was sent over to go along for backup, in case I got shot in the mouth or something.

Things went along that way for a while until one day when we slipped down a draw where there were trees for cover. We got along for a mile or so and hadn't been seen it seemed, but we were just climbing out of a gully to head up a hill when someone about half way up that hill opened up on us with a machine gun. Most dived back in the gully but five were blown back, and lay pretty still. Slim and I gave them a quick check over but didn't find any pulse or heartbeat, and they were not breathing; so we couldn't do much in the line of helping them.

My heart raced on ahead of me as I cranked on the field telephone and said, "*Toka oyasin oksan unkiyepi* (Enemy all around us). *Opawinge wikcemna ekta mazaskanskan wikcemna* (One thousand at ten o'clock), *opawinge wikcemna kin nunpa moccasins* (two thousand feet), *itkonza at mazaskanskan nunpa* (same at two o'clock)." Before we had left, we had been told the Germans weren't taking prisoners much, so giving up would probably just get us shot, and I for one would rather be shot than be a prisoner. I had had enough of that before I came to the army. The chances of us holding out until reinforcements got there were slimmer than the chances of a chunk of ice on a red hot stove. Some of the guys started praying. I thought it might be a little late for me to start praying, but it was time for some action.

Felix was trying to tie a white hanky on his rifle—I motioned to him to wait. I crawled down the gully out of sight of the machine gunner, got behind a tree, and shinnied up it about twenty feet in less than a jiffy. I took aim at a German behind the machine gun—as soon as he fell over, another one grabbed the machine gun and I popped him, too. They kept stepping up and I kept knocking them down. After about six knockdowns, there just wasn't any more Germans at the machine gun, so I slid back down the tree and headed up the hill at top speed. No one shot at me, and when I reached the machine gun, there were six dead German soldiers, but none alive. The rest of the platoon were soon right there with me. The platoon sergeant hoisted up the machine gun, and we went leaps and bounds for the top of the hill. We must have looked mighty fierce, because there were half a dozen German lads who just left their rifles on top of the hill. When we got there, we saw them running like a herd of scared rabbits down the other side.

"Well, you just never know, but it sure looks like a better vantage point than it did a few minutes ago!" I said to Felix as I handed him the phone set. "Your turn to talk to battalion."

Very shortly he was telling them (in Lakota), "We've secured this hill, but there's still at least a battalion of Germans to the west and another to the east of us."

It wasn't long before we heard the big guns, and we watched as round after round hit right in the midst of both of the German battalions. It looked like mass confusion was running wild in both German camps. We soon had German soldiers coming at us from both sides waving white flags. Some Germans did retreat, but we captured several hundred. As we were walking back down that hill, I said to one of the soldiers who had been praying, "Maybe it does help to pray." It had been a long day.

As new troops came in, we were moved more to the east on the line, and we were about to cross the bridge on the Somme River—a stronghold the Germans dearly hated to give up—but they did. We had been at this little war for over two months now with no end in sight yet. The French and British were sure glad to see us. They had been at this war going on three years before we got involved, and now we were like a breath of fresh air to them. We had come along at the right time to stop the Germans from overrunning the whole country.

We finally got some time off and got paid and had a chance to write home. I sent half my pay home in a letter to Lizzy. And, we finally had a mail call. Most of us got some mail, but some of the names called off weren't there to receive their mail, and never would be—they had met a bullet or grenade somewhere along the way. It made for an eerie feeling with me, because I had witnessed some of their fate, and even tried to revive a few. Slim had gotten a whole bundle of letters, mostly from Alma. There must be a spark of love between them two. Sure hate to see him get shot. Already I caught him with his back to a gun on more than one occasion. His chances of surviving until we got out of there looked pretty slim, but on the other hand, no one's chances of surviving this little skirmish looked real good.

CHAPTER 4

After We Seen Paris

The war stretched on, but things started looking up. Most of us had just been promoted to Private First Class, and we got a three-day pass, so we decided to take a train over to the big city of Paris. We could be there in about four hours, and it didn't cost much for a round-trip ticket. The French money was called francs, and we could buy about seven francs for a dollar, so things seemed cheap in France. One of the French soldiers who was in our group spoke English, too, so we had us a guide and translator. We were off and heading for a wild weekend. Paris looked a little ragged. A lot of the buildings were blown apart, but there were a great many buildings and most were still intact. The train station was bombed pretty bad but was still functional. The Germans would fly a bunch of airplanes low over the city and throw out bombs where they thought it would do the most good on places like the train station and anything that looked like an ammunition dump. We were all soon following our "guide" down a street. We went a few blocks, then he took us into a good sized tavern, where we could eat, drink, and make merry if we wanted to.

Harry, Slim, and I chose to eat, so we had our translator tell the innkeeper to bring us a steak with all the trimmings. Most of the guys just bellied up to the bar and started sampling the French spirit waters, but some did go right up the stairs with "Marie." It wasn't long and we had a big plate of food with a huge round steak right in the middle. It was good meat, sweet tasting, and real pink looking, but I was sure it wasn't beef or buffalo. After we were done eating, I asked the Frenchman, "What kind of meat was that?"

"*La viande de cheval.* We have very good *cheval*!" he said gesturing with hands in an up and down riding motion.

Harry looked a little greenish all the sudden, and said, "Does that mean horse? I didn't know I could eat a horse. At home, horses are too important to just eat them. If I'd known, I guess I'd rather gone hungry."

I thought it over and said, "Somebody once said to me when in Rome, do as the Romans do. So just do as the French." It took a while before he lost that greenish color.

We found a boarding house and got a room for the night. Slim, Harry, and I then decided to walk around the town a little. The people were sure friendly—most couldn't speak any English—but they wanted to shake our hands, and some even gave us a hug and kissed us on the cheeks. I didn't go much for some old duff kissing me on the cheek, but they meant well. We had been strolling along for a few blocks when kind of suddenly I noticed an arm slipping around my waist, and there was a very pretty gal attached to it. Slim and Harry each had a pretty gal walking with them too. This brought us to a screeching halt. When we stopped, the girls gave us hugs and said "Aloe, Aloe." I thought it must mean "hello," so I said "Aloe." This brought a giggle from the girls, and we had real French guides for the weekend. They couldn't speak English or Indian and we couldn't speak French, but we were willing to try to learn. We did a lot of talking with our hands and pointing, and we learned that some things are just universal.

We all made it back to camp and in a lot better spirits than a few days ago—some of the boys really had hangovers. Very shortly we were back in the combat zone. This time Snooky and I were summoned to the battalion commander's tent. The front had advanced up close to a little burg called Cantigny. We were supposed to sneak into that town and bring back a report on what we found. Sounds simple enough, I thought, but, I already knew, things can get complicated in a fast hurry. I said to Major Bates, "Sure would like to have a pistol like the one you're wearing to take with me."

He unbuckled his pistol belt, handed it to me, and said, "Be sure to give it back when you get out of Cantigny. And watch yourselves—the last three recons we sent in didn't make it back."

We headed into the town at nighttime to have a better chance of not being seen. The houses were all dark. The windows had been painted black, but we could still see a faint light around the edges of some of them. Some of the houses were beyond windows—there had been a lot of shells dropped on this town from both sides. Snooky was walking in front down an alley that was really dark. A door opened right in front of me and I almost walked into it. Someone grabbed my arm and jerked me inside quick as a flash and shut the door. There was a dim light in the background somewhere, and I could make out the figure of a woman right in front of me.

She said, in a very low voice, and in English, "I am a friend to you Americans, and I want to help you. Please beckon your buddy to come in and we will talk." I stepped back outside and Snooky was right there, so I just grabbed his arm and stepped back inside. "It is not safe here, but we have a hideaway room in the back where we can talk," she said. Without another word we all three headed for her back room. She closed the door and said, "I am Rosa Schmidt. I studied at the university in Cologne and was just starting my practice there as a doctor when the war started. I left to come home to Belgium to be with my parents, but we were not safe in Ypres—there was much fighting—so we came to try to find safety in France. At home we speak German as do many Belgians, but also we speak French, and I learned English at the university. I have seen many horrible things that Kaiser Wilhelm's German soldiers have done to our people. That is why I will do anything I can to help the other side win this war. What is it you want to know?"

We introduced ourselves, then, I told her we needed to find out where and how many German soldiers were in this town. She said, "That is easy, I do rounds each day at their hospital or sick bay. It is right in the center of the town, and the German soldiers occupy all the houses to the west, east, and north of the hospital. They only have a small number here now, but I overheard some officers talking this morning about a large advance of troops coming in two days, then they plan a massive attack. I think they said over twenty thousand more soldiers will be here day after tomorrow, and more will follow shortly if they are needed. Russia has made a treaty with Kaiser Wilhelm, so all the German soldiers that were over there are now being sent to the Western Front."

"That is a lot of information, but somehow we will need to make sure of it," I said.

"I have a plan," said Rosa. "One of you will wrap a blanket over your shoulders and pretend to be sick, and I will walk along holding you up. If we are stopped by any German guards, I have a doctor's pass and can go anywhere anytime, so I will just say you are Peter Goloski and you are sick and I am taking you to the hospital. Peter is a neighbor friend of mine, and you, Private Gilland, look a lot like him. In the dark you should be able to pass. Do you have a better plan?"

I said, "Not really."

"Strip off," Rosa commanded, and she handed me a robe and a pair of slippers.

"If it is going to work, we have to make it look real." Then she handed me a belt and said, "You can stick your pistol in front of you in this. If we get caught, please, shoot me, too. I would rather be dead than a prisoner to these German soldiers."

I was slouched over with a blanket around me trying to look really sick, and Rosa was doing her part, when a German soldier stepped in front of us and said, "Halt!" I knew what that meant.

Rosa said, *"Guten Abend,"* then she showed him her card, and continued in German, "This is Peter Goloski, and I am taking him to the hospital. He is very sick."

The soldier said something that might have been an offer of help, but Rosa replied, *"Nein Danke,"* and I knew that meant no thanks.

The soldier said, *"Guten Abend,"* and stepped aside.

We were on our way again, and I didn't have to shoot her. I sure hoped Snooky was safe in that "safe" room and waiting for our return. This Rosa was sure one hell of a woman—we could have both been shot just then if she hadn't kept her cool. We walked right past the hospital and on down the street and headed back down another dark street and back to Rosa's place. We didn't get stopped anymore, but I for one was sure glad to get back into my clothes again. I thanked Rosa before we got out of the building. "Maybe we'll meet again when things are different," I added. Snooky and I headed back to camp.

We made it back to battalion commander's tent and reported all we knew about the situation firsthand. Then Snooky got on the field telephone and told the Signal Corps soldier at headquarters in Lakota what we had seen. At the other end of the line, there was a Lakota from the Pine Ridge area, who translated Snooky's report back into English for General Pershing's staff. That was one code the Germans couldn't break, and nobody had to carry around a code book!

Our commanding officer, Major Winfred Werpel said, "You boys go on over to the officer's tent. Take the first empty bunks you find and get some sleep." Major Werpel had been born in Germany but came to the United States with his parents at an early age; he'd joined the US Army and gone to officer's school. It was more near morning than midnight, so he didn't have to tell us twice.

It seemed like I just got to sleep, when I heard shooting and a lot of it. That ended the good night's sleep. Our tanks and big guns hit Cantigny with everything we had, right up the middle and around both sides. Before evening of the second day, we had secured the town and were advancing on past it. There had been plenty of casualties, so I had my job back again, at least temporary, and was out at the field hospital—just a bunch of tents set up for treating the wounded. It sure seemed safer than it had back in Rosa's little "safe" room. I thought this war is going to last, and last, and last. I was deep in thought, when one of the orderly's yelled, "Gilland, you're wanted over at the doctor's tent."

Now what? I headed on over to the doctor's tent and stepped inside. There facing me was a very pretty woman with a white doctor's cloak—Rosa. She was much better looking in the daylight. "Hello my sick friend," she said and came right to me and gave me a big hug and a kiss right on the mouth! I didn't even have time to resist, not that I would have anyway.

"You kind of surprised me. I sure wasn't expecting to see you," I said.

"I'm a doctor you know," she said, "Helping out here seemed like the least I could do, and there has been plenty of work to go around. But your officer said that I could take you home with me tonight as long as you are back here by eight o'clock in the morning. A warm clean bed to sleep in, and my mother will have a real home-cooked meal ready for us when we get there. She is a very good cook. Of course, if you would rather stay here and sleep on the ground and eat army rations, that's up to you."

What a choice! I said, "No one can beat a deal like that, let's go." Rosa's mother met us at the door and was all smiles, but I soon learned that she didn't speak any English. We were sitting at the table and there were only three places set. I remembered Rosa had said she had come home to help her parents, so I asked, "Isn't your father going to join us?"

Rosa's face darkened as she said, "No, Papa was shot by a German soldier almost two years ago. He was helping some people get away from the soldiers and was caught. That was one of the reasons I had to help you get the soldiers out of here." We all brightened up after a fantastic meal. I wasn't too sure what it was, but it was certainly good. Rosa said, "Let us go for a walk, and this time you do not have to pretend to be sick." The people on the streets were real friendly, and I think all of them knew Rosa. We walked quite a while, and it was getting near dark by the time we got back to the house. Rosa's mother had already gone to her room. Rosa took me to the only other bedroom and said, "Here is that clean bed I promised," and slipped out of her clothes and slid into bed, "I'll warm it up for you."

"*Guten Morgan, Rosa. Fr hst ck ist fertig* (Good Morning, Rosa. Breakfast is ready)," said Rosa's mother with a gentle knock on the door. We had a hot breakfast and the strongest hot coffee. I thought that my brother Ben back home made strong coffee, but his would not hold a candle to this, and it was good.

Then I went off to work. We were plenty early, but there was no shortage of work for a medic. The front was slowly advancing and we had a lot of casualties. The weather was getting cold now, too, and we were treating lots of frostbite and rotten feet, mostly from being in wet and muddy trenches. Most of the soldiers were spending days in the trenches and only had one pair of dry socks extra in their haversacks. There was no hanging anything out to dry. It rained a lot on the French-German border. If it wasn't raining, it was at least cloudy. We hardly ever seen the sun, and if we did, it was only for an hour or so and then back to drizzling. Now the drizzle was getting mixed with snow. I thought, "What a place to fight for."

A steady flow of new recruits was coming in now, and we old recruits finally got another three days off. We got paid again, and we even got mail from home. Getting mail from home was always the big event around our camp, and it spread a little hope in a dim situation. Bess wrote that she was pregnant and expecting in January. She said that Dad was drinking more than was good and Mother had took the axe and chopped the spokes out of Dad's buggy to keep him from going to town. I figured Mother must have had enough and took care of things in her own way. Liz wrote that she was expecting a baby around the first of December. That meant that I was more than likely the baby's father. She was still with the man her father forced her into marrying, but he must have figured the child wasn't his. She wanted to stay in Mobridge, close to a doctor. Her husband was drunk all the time anyway and just left her alone—he often left for days at a time. Phoebe had been staying with her, and she had enough money saved up to get a place of her own as soon as the baby was born. She said she sure hoped I'd get myself home! This time I sent all my pay home to Lizzy. I still had money from last time, and there just wasn't a lot to spend money on in these parts.

I shared a pup tent with Slim. He had gotten several letters from his gal south of Thunder Hawk, and she had told him all about the good crops they had just harvested and all the other little happenings at Thunder Hawk. We were just lying there wondering what we were going to do when Snooky stuck his head in. "Come on, you guys, we're having a poker game over in the mess tent and we need some new money in the game." He laughed, "Bring your cache."

Slim asked, "Should we go win his money?"

"Well, why not!" I said. So we were off to win our fortunes. We only played for a nickel ante, and a dime limit on a raise with a three raise limit, so we could play for hours and maybe win or lose three or four dollars, but it sure whittled away an evening. We had played for over five hours and I was getting tired, so I suggested that we play showdown and quit. (Showdown was, everyone threw in fifty cents, and the dealer turned everyone's card face up and the top hand took the pot.) So showdown it was, and Slim was the winner, but I had about three dollars in extra change, so Slim and I headed back to our tents feeling kind of good about our winnings.

We were already starting a new year and still holding the front. Mail came but there was no letter from Liz. I thought that was odd, but maybe she had the baby and was just too busy to write or maybe there were complications and she was too sick to write—the possibilities were a lot. But there was a letter from my brother Ben and I thought that is even more odd as he has never wrote since I have been over here. I opened his letter and read:

Dear Bob,

I hate to have to tell you this bad news, but I know you have to know. Liz had her baby. It's a boy, and she named him after you, but when she was home getting ready to leave for good, that drunk SOB she was married to came in. When he seen she was getting ready to leave, he went into a mad rage and started beating on her. Phoebe grabbed up the baby and ran for help, but when they got there, Liz was beat so bad she was barely alive. They got her to the hospital as soon as possible, but she was bleeding inside bad, and she died. There just wasn't anything anyone could do. I'm so damned sorry.

I heard she was moving over to McIntosh, and I figured everything was fine. Had I had even a slight notion that she was living in danger, I would have went over there and escorted her out of there myself. Some of us went looking for that bastard, but they had whisked him off to jail, and then he got sent to Leavenworth, Kansas, but his life won't last long if we can ever find a way to get to him. The court said you were not in a position to raise a child with your criminal record, and they thought it best to just put your son up for adoption. They took the boy from Phoebe, but we are all trying to get the court to let someone in the family raise your son.

Your brother,

Ben

I had heard about Dear John letters that some of the guys had gotten since they were here, but, boy, this was the granddaddy of them all. I couldn't sleep that night. I just kept thinking of all the things I should have done differently. I could have done a lot more, and finally I reached a conclusion: fate had dealt me a bad hand but it is how you play your cards that counts. I couldn't bring Liz back, no matter what. But I could make sure the guy who had killed her got the same treatment.

I had made a few friends at Leavenworth when I was there and any one of a dozen or more would gladly do me a favor. Big John, especially. No one knew Big John's name, and if they spoke to him at all it was "Big John." I had shared a cell with him and we got along great. He liked me and just acted like I was his little brother. The first night there at Leavenworth, I was put in a cell with Big John. Along about midnight (the inner cell doors were left open so we could all walk down the hall and use the one latrine on that cell block), I was still wide awake. Big John had just went to the latrine, and three guys came runnin' in and one of them said, "Injun, we are all horny as hell and you is going to be our sweet ass tonight."

I said, "Not in your lifetime." I peeled out of bed and hit the one who had spoken just as hard as I could. He went back hard and hit the floor. The other two were grabbing at my arms, when Big John walked in. He took a guy by the back of the neck in each hand and rammed them as hard as he could face first into the cell bars and without letting go threw them down the hall. Then he reached down and picked up the one lying on the floor and smashed him into the cell bars too, and gave him a fling out in the hall.

He closed the cell door and turned and said, "No one is going to corn hole anyone in my cell." Then added, "We better get to bed pronto, before a guard comes looking to see what the racket was about." I was in my bed and (at least pretending to sleep) in less than two seconds. The next morning the guard came around and found those three horny dinks still lying in the hall, cold and dead. The guards sure started asking a lot of questions.

"I didn't hear or see anything," I told the guards, "I was tired and I went right to sleep and never woke up until just now." No one else talked either. Big John just gave them a mean glare, and the guards didn't even ask him a thing. They put me in solitary confinement for ten days trying to make me talk, but I figured I'd rather eat bread and water for ten days than try to explain to Big John as to why I talked. After ten days, the guards finally gave up on me talking and just put me back in with Big John. He soon started talking to me and even told me his real name. I wouldn't even tell my own mother his name because that is the way he wanted it.

"I've mined coal, done a few years as a lumberjack, and worked on the railroad for a while," he told me. "I had to quit that job though. One day the crew had to unload a load of eight-feet oak ties and carry them ways down the track. They had been just carrying one tie each. Then the foreman said to double up on carrying those ties, so I carried two at a time for a while. Then that foreman said take five, so I carried five. But the second bunch of five, I just threw 'em down at the foreman's feet and quit. Damned if I was gonna carry that many."

I wasn't sure if he was just kidding or if he really did carry that many ties, but I thought if anyone could, it most likely would be Big John. He had said he had gotten life for killing a few skunks in a fight, and I left it at that. But we soon became good friends and he had said when I was about to leave, "If ever I can do anything for you, just let me know."

I wrote "Big John" and the address (I still remembered it well) on an envelope and just sent him Ben's letter. I thought when Big John gets this letter that skunk's chances of surviving a night in that jail is slimmer than a mouse's in a pen of rattlesnakes.

CHAPTER 5

The German Lines

We had been on the front a year, and the war was fast getting to be old news. We were not gaining a lot of ground in a hurry. It was a slow progress, and we had to fight dearly for every foot we gained. But we were on the move again—this time we were sent to a place called Belleau Wood. We packed up and left without fair warning. I didn't even have a chance to say *Auf Wiedersehen* (Good-bye until we meet again) or *Danke schön* (Thank you) to Rosa. Our whole company was convoyed down to near Belleau Wood with orders to head for the front line.

The Germans had been hitting that area hard, and the battalion needed to send a recon patrol out right shortly to try to pinpoint German strongholds. Twenty of us got picked, and Harry and I got selected as the "Indian talkers." Slim and Earl were in our bunch, too. It was midsummer already, so the weather had warmed up quite a bit, but the clouds and rain were still with us on the night we moved out. We headed out right after dark and it was a foggy night. We crawled right through the enemy line—we could see a sentry sitting up, but it looked like he was sound asleep and we didn't go over and wake him. It was darker than hillbilly hell, but that was to our advantage. After around a mile of crawling and tiptoeing, along with stringing along our communication wire, we seen some dim lights ahead. We stayed to the right of the lights and tippy-toed until we saw more dim lights and could make out a lot of tents and even several rows of Big Bertha guns. That's what the Germans called their new and very big long-range piece of artillery. The guns were a lot bigger than any artillery howitzers the Allied forces had, but we had tanks with big guns on them. The tanks could go right through about anything and right over that damnable concertina wire.

The farther we went, the more we seen of German tents and equipment. The fog was breaking a little, and we could see the outline of a hill against the skyline maybe a quarter mile just east of us; so we headed for it. We were coming up in the dark and they couldn't see us, but we could see two fellows walking back and forth on that hilltop. Nothing was said, but Earl and Slim with bayonets in hand handed someone else their rifles and headed up the hill. The German guards were about ten feet apart with their backs to each other when suddenly two figures dived in behind them and their guard duty was soon ended. The figures disappeared from sight, so we all headed on up the hill. When we got up to the hill, we saw the German soldiers both had their throats cut. They were still kicking a little, but Slim and Earl had a hand over their mouths. They weren't going anywhere and they sure didn't make a sound.

We had trailed up telephone wires and handsets as far as we could. We were soon talking Indian to battalion and gave the details of what we had seen. We got orders back to just dig in and wait for the fireworks to begin.

"Kawam!" A burst of fire hit the German camp and lit up the sky. Then there was howitzer rounds hitting all around us.

"Snooky, are you sure you made it clear which hill we're on?" I asked. When a round hit close to us, we could see German soldiers scrambling in every direction.

Our platoon leader Duane Frey said, "Be ready boys, no doubt we'll have unwanted company before we get off this hill." He was right! There were Germans coming at us from every direction but down. There was enough firepower that the whole area around us was lit up most of the time. We had to start shooting. We kept shooting and they kept coming. It seemed like hours, but it was probably more like a few minutes (in all the excitement you sort of lose track of time).

About a hundred yards over, I seen Slim bent over a soldier lying on the ground. I could see a lot of red on his right leg, and Slim was trying to look and see how bad he was bleeding. A bullet hit the dirt alongside of me, then another over the soldier lying on the ground. That time I seen where it had come from, and I could still see his helmet. They said I could shoot back if someone was shooting at me and I wasn't treating a wounded. I could shoot—Slim was too busy to even notice the bullets hitting around him—so I just fired my rifle from the hip like I would have if I'd had my pistol. It stung my hand pretty good, but it worked; the shooter went out of sight and didn't shoot again.

I got to Slim and said, "Let me get on one side and let's pull your patient up ahead to a little shelter." Slim just nodded, and we had that lad up behind a bank in a lot less time than half a minute. The soldier had just a flesh wound through the upper right leg, but it was to one side and didn't hit any big arteries; so his wound wasn't bleeding a lot. I helped Slim bandage the soldier's leg.

"I'm ready to go on if you just help me get on my feet," the soldier said. We did better than that, we got him to his feet, then I swung one of his arms over my neck, and Slim did the other one, and we ran up and over that hill in a split jiffy. Major Werpel already had a perimeter established and was snapping orders at everyone who came into camp. There were already several soldiers lying on the ground under some trees, and he waved us toward them. We joined the other medics there. Mostly we made it, only lost nine soldiers and nineteen wounded, but a few of the wounded very likely wouldn't see another sunrise.

As Slim and I checked over the men lying in the field, we came upon a terrible sight. When we turned over a mud-covered soldier who was lying face down, it was Felix. Just lying there with his mouth open but not a scratch on him. The blast from the Big Bertha shells sometimes did that. It blew a man up into the air and crushed his brains not with bullets but with noise. We sat for a long while with Felix, closed his mouth and his eyes, and tried without words to honor our fallen brother. I searched for the Lakota words that would help rest his soul. Felix would be buried in a French cemetery as a stranger in this foreign land. He would be honored as a hero here one day, but his mother and father would only have a telegram. There would be no war songs, no victory songs, no home-coming parade with Felix leading the way.

"This war will be harder going, much harder without you old friend. *Ake wancinyanking ktelo* (Farewell, I'll see you again one day)."

It was getting to be daylight. There wasn't as many Germans trying to climb our hill, but we still had to keep a sharp eye. Our ammunition was getting really low. I thought we should have brought more. If we ran out of shells, it would be hand-to-hand combat. I hoped I remembered how to use a bayonet. I knew my worries were unfounded when we saw the tanks coming up from be-hind us with a lot of our soldiers right behind them. The Germans gave up on wanting to come up this hill and started running pretty fast in the other direction. We had had gained some territory and sure put a dent in that German army and silenced quite a few of their Big Berthas.

We didn't have to go back to camp though, instead camp came to us that day. My mouth felt like cotton, and it felt like my backbone was rubbing on my belly button. I was both thirsty and hungry, so I drank half of my canteen of water and dug out some C-rations from my backpack and chowed down. The sun had come out and it was warm. Some of the guys had already used their packs for pillows and were sleeping on the side of that hill, so I did the same. We may have been asleep for a little over half an hour when someone down the hill yelled "Medic, medic." I sat up kind of star-tled, and Slim did too. There down the hill about fifty feet was a young recruit, looking all excited. He had seen us all lying on that hillside and thought we were dead. When we sat up, he sure had a dumb look on his face. Slim said, "Should I shoot him or do you want to?" The thought was tempting, but I didn't.

The war dragged on. After about a month, we got paid and we got another break with a whole week to get rested up. This time I didn't feel much like writing letters, so I caught a ride with the ammunition truck to Cantigny. (They made the run back and forth every day, so I could catch a ride back too. We could get fired at from the enemy but I thought, who cares.) There was still a field hospital at Cantigny, and Rosa was still helping out, but she had already gone home by the time I got there, so I just went over to her house and knocked on the door. Rosa's mother came to the door. When she saw me, she grabbed me and gave me a big hug, then pulled me inside, and said, "*Guten Abend* (Good Evening). *Rosa ist zum Market gegangen* (Rosa is out to the market). *Komm herein, komm, komm* (Come, come)." She pointed to a soft chair. By then, I knew a few words of German and could tell she was glad to see me. I had picked up about half a duffel bag of different C-rations at camp. Rosa had told me before that the people were really having hard times and a little food went a long way with them.

"*Das ist für dich* (This is for you)," I said and handed her the duffel bag.

"*Danke, danke* (Thank you, thank you)," she said as she took the bag right to the kitchen. I sat down and just waited, but in a few minutes, in walked Rosa. She looked at me like she didn't believe what she saw, then quickly came right over and I got a big hug.

"You really surprised me! It is good to see you again, but you are not much at saying good-bye!" she said.

"I didn't know we were even leaving until we were told to grab our bags and rifles and load up. Not much chance of saying good-byes with orders like that," I said.

"Oh, I know. I'm sure glad you are back, but I was hoping to get a letter from you," she added.

"There wasn't any post offices where I was at," I said.

"I was just over to the market, but there isn't much food to be bought. I'm sure Mother will have plenty fixed for supper though," she said changing the subject. We walked into the kitchen and her mother had a fantastic meal on the table. Rosa was surprised again.

Three days later, my leave was over, but it sure had boosted my moral. I caught the ammo truck again and back to camp I went. We were off to fight another battle. I thought, "I'm a medic, I'm not supposed to be an infantry man. And this going out ahead of the front lines and calling reports back in Indian is for the birds.

I'd sure a lot rather be back in Dakota on the reservation shooting at gophers with my pistol from a running horse rather than at these German soldiers."

CHAPTER 6

The Eleventh Hour of the Eleventh Day

We were at a place called Verdun. The Germans had really put up a fight to hold this area, but they were slowly losing ground. Humba, humba, tadalaa, tadalaa, tadalaa, humba, tadalaa, tadalaa, tadalaa beat a drum with a bunch of German soldiers singing in cadence a little before noon. A whole company of German soldiers came marching right across the front line at us carrying a white flag, marching to the beat of the drum with their hands on their heads. They weren't carrying any rifles, so no one shot at them. They marched right up in front of the commanding officer's tent and halted in formation. I thought, "Wow, that's the way to capture prisoners. It's a lot easier than trying to roust them out of the bushes!"

The German line was weakening all along the front, and by the grapevine we heard rumors of the German army being overrun in other parts of the battlefield as well. One of Germany's allies, Bulgaria, had just surrendered, so there was new hope for this war to end soon. This news really gave new spark to the Allied forces, but there was a big concentration of German forces at a place called St. Mihiel, and that was our next stop. This time, only we medics were sent. I thought, "Hopefully, I won't have to do anymore of their Indian talking. It was supposed to just be a temporary job, anyway, but it had already lasted more than a year. We had our hands full at St. Mihiel, casualties were coming in faster than we could keep up treating them, and the battle raged on."

They announced over the loudspeaker one day that more of Germany's allies had surrendered—Turkey and Austria-Hungary. The war looked like it was coming to a close, but here, out in front of us, it was still going strong.

A little past noon, on November 11, we heard church bells ringing in all the burgs around us, and whistles and sirens. "An armistice has just been signed. The war is over," boomed a voice over the loudspeaker, The Germans had just signed an armistice in a town called Compiegne, France. There was sure a lot of happy fellows at camp now! Even the faces of wounded soldiers had a happy look.

We had payday again, and now we had good reason to celebrate. We had mail call too, and I had a letter from Dad. Mother couldn't write and Dad never did, so I thought it must be something pretty drastic. I opened the letter dreading to read it, but I did. Dad was brief:

There has been a flu epidemic of some kind going around here and a lot of people have died from it. Ben was one of them on the 18th of October. He had been sick for several days. One morning he got up, dressed himself, and put his boots on. He went out and walked around his cabin, when he came back in he lay down on the bed and died.

Damned luck! He was always the toughest one in the family. How could he just die from a flu? Ben always said he would die with his boots on, and I guess he got his wish. Bess wrote too, and she gave all the details about Ben. She said that Alice (Lizzy's oldest sister) had gotten custody of Robert Junior. A lot of people had died from the flu. So many that some were buried on hills near their homesteads, because the undertakers just couldn't keep up, and people were afraid to go near the dead for fear of catching the flu. She wrote that apart from the flu epidemic, they were doing as well as could be expected and the hay and grain crops had been good. And one other thing that might be of interest to me she said that fellow who had beat up Liz was found in his cell down at Leavenworth just beat to death. The *Lemmon Leader* said that they couldn't find out who did it, but they thought more than a dozen inmates had taken part. He had been beaten so bad that he wasn't even recognizable.

I silently said, "Thanks, Big John. I knew I could count on you!"

We would soon be back on that old boat and heading home. My feelings about going home were sort of mixed up. Liz was my main reason for going home, and without her there, there sure would be a big void in my life. And without Ben, it would be very different. I thought, "Maybe I should just stay over here and marry Rosa and help rebuild her country." That would be the smart thing to do, but I never was much good at doing the smart thing. And I still had hopes of being a successful rancher back on the reservation. That is what I grew up with and knew best, and I liked that way of life. If I stayed here, I would most likely get a job working at a hospital as a medic, and I had done that back in the states, and I was sick of it in less than three weeks. If I stayed here, I would have to learn to talk German, but that wouldn't be too hard. The way you spoke a sentence in German was very much like the Lakota language. (I had learned that much from talking with Rosa.) If I stayed here, though, very likely I would never see any of my family again, and that in itself would be a bit hard. I thought, "I should be off to spend my last days here with Rosa, but, then, if I'm not staying, it wouldn't be fair to her. Now that the war is over we could finally talk about our future together." No, I decided, it would be better to just leave and let Rosa find a good Belgian man, and she surely could, she was one of the most attractive gals I had ever seen. I never was much good at saying good-bye, anyway.

Some of the troops were being sent home right away, but our dear President Woodrow Wilson had decided to keep a strong force in France for six months, just in case the armistice wasn't honored. And, of course, our company was one of the lucky ones getting to stay. Now we had to help undo some of the things we worked so hard to do. There was a lot of filling in of trenches and craters and cleaning up in general, and when I wasn't needed as a medic, I was sent with the boys to help out. At least I was relieved of my "temporary" Indian talking job that had lasted for well over a year.

We had been relocated to somewhere near Soissons, a little town north of Paris. One day we were out filling in trenches and I was amazed at how anyone could have dug in like we did. In that ground, it took hours with a pick and shovel just to fill in some of those holes. It was hard to believe anyone could have dug them in just minutes, sometimes it looked like they had been dug with bare hands. It made me think, the strength of a scared man is mighty! Then, there were endless miles of concertina wire to clean up. Germany had sent some soldiers to help too—now we were working side by side with German soldiers. I thought, "It's sure a lot better than shooting at each other." Some of the German soldiers were mere boys of fifteen or sixteen; they must have been running pretty short on fighting age men.

At last we are marching up the ramp to board our ride home. It didn't take long, and we were rolling on the waves and heading for New York Harbor. The ocean wasn't nearly as rough going back as it was coming over, and we didn't have nearly as many seasick sailors this time.

New York City was quite a sight. There were buildings higher than I had ever imagined, and for every building, there must have been a thousand people. We had three days before we had to catch a train out to a place called Camp Zackary Taylor in Kentucky, to get discharged and then sent back to Thunder Hawk, South Dakota, and the green, green grass of home! A few of us were getting about three-fourths anxious to get home, especially, a tall slim fellow walking into New York City with me. I suspect he had Alma on his mind. A few days of taking in the sights of New York, army style, and we just made it to the train heading to Camp Zackary Taylor. We stayed there long enough to get discharged on July 29, 1919. We were two happy ex-combat veterans heading for home.

When we got to Kansas City, Slim's folks and four brothers and a sister were there. His mother had been sickly as of late, so Slim said he was going to stay in Missouri for a while before coming back to Thunder Hawk. He said, "From here on out, you will just have to look out for yourself."

"Well," I said, "you've done a good job at keeping us both alive the last couple of years. Thanks, my friend!" Then I was on my own, heading for Thunder Hawk, and, I hoped, a better chapter in my life. I was unsure as to how much of my old life there would be the same and how much would have been changed by the war. I know I had been changed.

CHAPTER 7

Harkening Back to Ben

"Go home and pick up life where you left it. Get on with your life and leave the war and the army behind you," said the officer at Camp Taylor in his mustering out speech when we got discharged. That sounded like good advice, and I was sure going to try to do as he said. But I knew some things would not be the same and some things can never be forgotten. I could not pick up with Lizzy where we left off—she was just not living in this world anymore. It would be hard to not have my brother Ben around.

My start in cattle and ranching was long gone, too. Most of the cattle and all of my land went pay for lawyers so that I could prove I didn't kill my cousin. I had drunk a lot of whiskey that night at the trail camp, but I couldn't remember shooting at Tom. In the army, I shot many a German soldier, and I remember every last one of them. I wish I could forget.

The train finally rolled into Thunder Hawk and home. With Lizzy and Ben both in my thoughts plenty, I stepped off the train. I thought too of Felix who would forever rest in a field in France and never be coming home to his family. I had been gone a long time with a lot train rides, a lot of experiences, and a lot of people gone by—some leaving deep memories and some not worth remembering at all. The town had sure grown while I was away. The station was jam-packed with people anxiously looking for others who were getting off the train, but right away I spotted Dad and Mother out of the crowd on the platform. My little brother Jimmy had grown up taller than me, and I guessed that I'd better call him Jim from now on. Bessie had her baby daughter in her arms and husband Charlie at her side.

"Welcome home son," Dad said softly as he shook my hand.

"Welcome home, *akicita* (soldier)," said Mother as she and Bessie both hugged me at the same time. Too many things had changed for me to pick up my life where I'd left off, but I sure was going to try to leave the army and the war behind me. As a first step, we were soon sitting down to a royal welcome and big supper at Samie Wong's Café. Samie was no longer the scared young boy Brave Bear and I had rescued from those low-life skunks in Montana. Now he was one of the upstanding citizens of Thunder Hawk. Folks came from all over to eat at Samie's. A good meal is always a good way to begin a new day.

Home at last! In my own bed, upstairs in our log house, just a mile east of Thunder Hawk, and it sure felt good. With the war over and no more army uniforms, I needed to get on with my life and get to making a living again. Before I got sent to Leavenworth before the war, I'd made a good start with my 320 acres, a small herd of cattle, and a few good horses. I lay there in bed thinking it is sure going to be different now. Homesteaders had moved in and set up on most nigh every quarter of land with barbed wire fences put up everywhere. Riding across the country was sure going to be a lot harder. The open range looked like something else belonging to the past.

After Ben died from the Spanish flu, Dad sold his homestead down south of the Grand River. I sure would miss Ben. We had many a good time together and a few wilder ones, too. Ben always seemed to know how to tell me how to do things I just couldn't quite get figured out. He always had good ideas, but sometimes they didn't work the way he had planned. Like when he decided to rope an antelope buck! One day when we were out riding, looking for cattle, we seen a big buck lying in the tall grass just over a grassy hill. It was real windy, and the antelope was just lying in the grass out of the wind.

Ben said softly, "Move back and forth slow like, and wave my bandana just enough to keep the antelope's attention. I'll slip around the back side of the hill; come over it wide open with my rope ready and rope the antelope before he can jump up and take off." Ben shot over that hill and was right on that antelope before it seen him. When it jumped up, Ben's rope was around its neck. That was the easy part—turning it loose got to be the problem. He tried walking down the rope and grabbing the buck, but that antelope would strike every time Ben got near him. He had on a new pair of chaps that he had ordered from one of those mail-order catalogs. They were real thin leather (goat hide I think), and that buck's hooves would cut them chaps every time it struck them and just ruined Ben's chaps.

Finally, he quit trying to turn it loose and just shot it with his 30-30, so he could get his rope off the cussed thing. Ben was a good shot with a pistol too, but he always said he could depend on his 30-30. He seldom missed with it. To watch him shoot it, you would think differently—he would weave around and the barrel would be moving an inch or two, but when he brought it down, he would hit whatever he was aiming at. Of course, then we had to dress out that antelope and pack it home so mother could can up the meat. Sure ended our looking for cattle that day.

Then there was the time Ben had sent away for a pair of spurs with two-inch Spanish rowels. "There is not a horse around that I can't ride with these spurs," he said not really boasting, just kinda matter of fact. This turned out to be a bit of an overstatement. I just had to watch. The first bronc Ben tried riding wearing those spurs threw him higher than a kite on about the third jump. He went straight up into the air. The Spanish rowels just rolled right up his saddle, and he rolled along and into midair. There were rowel marks up both stirrup fenders on his saddle. He got up, dusted himself off, took those spurs off, and walked right over to the creek bank and gave them a fling.

Ben's ideas didn't work out as planned either when he ordered some fruit trees of different kinds to plant on his homestead. He planted the trees just as the directions said and even watered them, but they all died. There were some Chinese matrimony bushes sent along as a bonus that he threw in the ash pile, and they grew. They are still growing all over that hillside.

Ben and I had broken a lot of horses together. Some of those horses made pretty fair riders out of us. Our neighbors Babe and his brother Bird Mansbridge thought they were some accomplished as riders too. The Mansbridge ranch was over southwest of the little town of Seim nestled into a clearing with big aspen and cottonwood trees around where the two branches of the Grand River came together. There were high banks to the north and south of the river about two miles to the south of Seim. Off one of those high banks was an old buffalo jump where our Lakota grandfathers used to run buffalo over banks to get their winter food supply. There were still hundreds of buffalo bones in the washed out area below that bank. When I was little, I had heard Dad talk about the time when old Ben Ash had a fight with a bear around there. He didn't do very good against the bear, but he did manage to crawl to Fort Pierre, so the story goes.

Ben had been over to Seim, and he and Babe had a few drinks too many, and they got to talking about how good they could ride. The annual rodeo at Seim was coming up in a few days. "Fifty bucks says that Bob and I can outride you and Bird," declared Ben. "We will let the judges' score at the rodeo settle the bet." We had been doing a few local rodeos, and we already knew how well the Mansbridge boys could ride. If we stayed sober and drew decent bucking horses, we would have a chance.

When the big day came, we were up early, put on our best shirts, and headed for Seim to make big money. I sure had butterflies. I didn't say anything to Ben, but I was thinking I wish he had left me out of his bet. There was a big crowd at Seim already when we got there even though the rodeo hadn't started yet. Ben had us entered up, but we had to draw for a horse to ride. Ike Blasingame and Louis Ducheaux had trailed over a rough stock bunch of horses that Ike said were buckers. I already knew if Ike said they were buckers, it was very likely an understatement. We had met Ike and Louis, who were from over on the Cheyenne Reservation, at several past cattle roundups, and several times they came and gathered their cattle off the Standing Rock Reservation; so we were pretty well acquainted. Ike was a white guy who rode for a big cattle out-fit, the Matador, and Louis was a breed with a cattle operation going over by John Dunbar's place. We used to try to hit Dunbar's place for a meal when we were rounding up in that area. They always welcomed company and especially breeds. They weren't Indian, but they spoke real good Lakota. John loved to talk and really told some pretty wild stories.

I drew a horse with the harmless sounding name of "Strawberry Roan." He was a beady-eyed, ugly son-of-a-gun, a red roan with a black mane and tail with plenty of buck in him. I managed to stay on for a qualified ride of ten seconds, but if I would have had to ride him to a standstill, I think I would have lost. I didn't have time to do a lot of fanning with my hat. Ike managed to come up with the highest score. He did a bang up job of fanning his horse with his hat, and he spurred well too. Babe placed second, Ben got third, I got fourth, and Bird managed to get fifth. Babe beat Ben by two points and I beat Bird by two points, so we had a standoff on their bet, but we all won a little money and we did a good job of spending it at Seim before we headed home. We could buy booze at Seim and at Sam Purdon's Place in Meadow, but the reservation was dry as far as Indians were concerned. There were around thirty other cowboys gathered in for the rodeo and quite a few others too who helped but didn't ride any broncos, so we had a good crowd to buy drinks for. We ran out of money about the time we were running out of night.

Ben sure knew how to handle horses. We had a dark bay that always pulled back and either broke the halter or the halter rope. Ben showed me how to put a stop to that. He set a post in the ground about ten feet out from the creek bank, just north of his homestead, and tied that horse to it. When that old pony started really pulling back, Ben just cut the halter rope. The dust flew and that horse really went back fast, and right over the bank; it was mostly straight down about twenty-five feet, and there was a big water hole below the bank. The horse went down the bank and hit the water on his back and sank into the water. Ben went down and caught him again when he came floundering out of the water. That sure took the pull out that horse—after that you could tie him with a shoe string and he wouldn't break it.

Then there was the paint that always kicked at everything that got close to his backside. Ben got tired of always shying around that horse when he was tied in the barn. So he hung a gunny sack of small rocks behind that horse's stall, about three feet off the floor of the barn. The horse was, at first, intent on kicking that sack out of the barn, but every time he kicked it, the sack would swing back and hit him in the rear. The horse was determined, but eventually the sack won the battle, and the horse gave up on his kicking habit.

Ben tried to teach me some about other things too. I had noticed that a lot of the boys used chewing tobacco, and I pestered him about what it was like. "Here, try this tobacco chew," he said without a hint of anything out of the ordinary in his voice. I was so sick that I never again had a craving to chew, and that was close to twenty years ago. Ben just helped me clean up and never said another word about chewing tobacco. Learning to mow hay was somewhat easier. The summer of 1902 Ben and I were putting up hay, and we stayed at our camp in our timber allotments along the river. Our log cabin, nestled in tall cottonwood trees with a high bank circled around to the east and south of our camp, was protected from winds from any direction. It had been a real scorcher of a day, and a heavy cloud bank had been building to the west for a couple of days. We had quit the hayfield early and had gone swimming in the river, but it was more like wading because the river wasn't running a lot and it wasn't easy to find a deep enough hole to swim in.

We had been in our beds for a few hours, but it was so hot and muggy I couldn't sleep much, and there wasn't a breeze from anywhere. To add to a miserable night, there was a steady rumble of thunder and a lot of lightning flashes. At first the rumble was at far distance, but as the night progressed, so did the thunder and lightning. Along about midnight, the wind suddenly came up with a mighty force and then the rain came. It rained hard for hours with the wind howling so loud it was more of a roar than a howl.

Daylight finally came and the rain and wind subsided as fast as it had started. Ben rolled out of the sack first, hollering over at me to get out of bed, then he said in a near hushed tone, "We better get outside and see if we still have any horses left. We need to get up to the mouth of Plum Creek and check on Chief Thunder Hawk and his camp there. That wind probably scattered those tepees to hell and breakfast." We hadn't slept much that night; at first light we were out saddling up a couple of horses and checking our camp. A few trees were not standing anymore, but mostly our camp weathered the storm. The storm had tipped over the hayrack, and the hay was mostly blown away.

Some of the people camped down on Plum Creek in the tepees were relatives and all were friends. We started getting anxious to check on the lot of them. The river was really raging, and we weren't real anxious to go swimming that day, so we rode west along the south side of the river. When we got close to the mouth of Plum Creek, we could see it looked pretty bad. Ben said just one word, "*Tah-teh-a-yo-m'ne* (cyclone)." We could see a large portion of a high bank along the west mouth of the creek was gone, and to the east of the creek, there was a pile of dirt that wasn't there before. The pile was ten feet high and maybe a hundred feet long and shaped like a huge grave. All the tepees were tipped over, torn apart, and some were completely gone. Stuff was scattered for miles, and people were trying to gather up some of their belongings. Some were hollering and some were silent. Three women were wailing, which was the Lakota way of mourning the death of a loved one, so we figured they were finding some who didn't survive the storm.

We had passed some of their ponies on our way over to the camp. Ben said, "Looks like they are in need of their horses. Let's go back and gather them up. Maybe the river will be going down again by the time we get them fetched." We headed out south, and in a mile or so, we came upon their horses. It didn't take much to get them headed back to the mouth of "Cyclone" Creek (that's what it was called after that day). The water had gone down about as fast as it had come up, and the horses went across with no problem. Chief Thunder Hawk and several others on the other side were catching the horses as we herded them in.

Seven people couldn't be found, and everyone figured they were buried under that mountain of dirt. We counted nine more bodies that were laid out covered with blankets, looked like mostly children. Ben and I set about helping to look for people. The first one we found was hanging in a tree about ten feet off the ground.

The young brave's braids were twisted around a branch and he was hanging by them. We managed to get him down, and he wasn't hurt much, but scared quite a bit. Another fellow had been blown into a thicket of willow trees and his back had big welts, just as if someone had whipped him with a bullwhip. Some of the people had gotten out of their tepees and into the trees and hung on to whatever they could grab in the dark. One woman said she was so scared that she just put her small child between her legs and just sat in the middle of the tepee with her shawl pulled over her head. When the storm stopped, she was still sitting there, but the tepee was gone along with a barrel of flour and her little cast iron cook stove.

After they buried the dead that weren't already buried in that giant grave, they got to loading up travois and were heading east as soon as they were able to. Chief Thunder Hawk had made summer camp at the mouth of Plum Creek for as long as I could remember. When the Indians had to move to the reservation, he had settled in this area but white man ways were slow coming to him. He and his little band of around twenty families, who were mostly his relations, still lived in tepees. Most were learning to talk some English from missionaries, and some of the younger ones had even gone to some schooling. The Indians in Thunder Hawk's group seemed to think *Tunka Wakon* (Great Spirit) didn't want them living in that area, and they were quick to oblige him by moving twenty miles downriver. Most would not even hunt in that area again.

There is a lot more I could tell about the times me and Ben had together, but if I had my druthers, I'd rather have him here with me. I'll always remember the good times and those that were on the funny side. Farewell Big Brother!

CHAPTER 8

Working the B-Bar-B Ranch

"Breakfast is on the table!" Dad hollered up. The night went fast, seemed like I just got to bed.

What a breakfast. Mother sure done us proud with her cooking—juneberry pancakes with thick cream and sugar sprinkled on, side pork cooked to perfection, and fresh homegrown eggs over easy just the way I liked them. Mother remembered everything I liked and just the way I liked it cooked. Jim was still a growing boy and it showed at the table. He was the first at the table to start eating, and he polished off the last two pancakes on the plate and kinda looked like he was beginning to slow on the eating a little when he was finished with them.

"I'll mix up another batch of sourdough and fry another dozen eggs if you boys will eat them," Mother offered in a pleasant voice.

"That was just the best breakfast, but I'm as full as a tick and couldn't eat another mouth full, but thanks," I said with a swallow. Jim still had a mouth full but shook his head no, so Mother just poured us another cup of coffee. Dad sat back in his chair and lit up his pipe. This morning even that pipe smoke smelled good like a sweet cherry tree burning.

He must have read my thoughts, because he said, "I switched to a new cherry blend tobacco. Mother tolerates it a little better than the other brand that I used to smoke. I get it from a Lakota friend who makes it from the inner bark of cherry trees.

"If you boys are looking for a job this morning, I just happen to know of one that will take up a day or two. The bank had some of the local boys gather up most of Ben's cattle. He had borrowed a little money from the bank to buy the cattle. Now, they said the other day that they had more than enough cattle to settle his debt, so they weren't going to look for anymore. Someone should gather up the rest of his cattle before winter sets in. I was thinking you boys would be good candidates for the job."

"I didn't come home to sit on the couch," I said as I looked over at Jim.

He looked across at me and said, "Let's get 'er done!" We loaded up a wagon and plenty of supplies, tied a couple of saddle horses on behind the wagon, and headed for the camp in our timber allotments down along the Grand River. There was a well-traveled road going south to the river now, and people were coming and going. I hadn't even imagined that so many people had moved into the area. Every quarter looked like it had a shack on it, and they all had a fence around the quarter. Some fences were a bit more elaborate than others, kind of like the shacks, in that respect. And each quarter had plowed patches or like the Indians would say the ground was turned wrong side up.

When we got close to the river, it became a little more sparsely settled, and there wasn't anyone close to our camp. The log house was pretty dusty and in dire need of a good cleaning, so that was the first thing we attended to. After a lick and a promise cleaning, we fixed up a fire in the stove and cooked some food. There was just about enough daylight left to patch up the corrals some, feed up the horses, and call it a day. Jim was a little new at this baching thing, but I had a feeling he would get the hang of it within the next fifty years or so. I couldn't help but wonder if Mother hadn't just spoiled him a tad bit. We went to bed early enough, but it was on the late side of the night before I ever dozed off. I kept remembering back when Ben and I had bached in this same cabin a dozen years or so ago. Things like, the time we played strip poker with the Duncan gals and I lost my shirt (that was the last time I ever played strip poker too). And the time Ben came back after a three-day drunk over at Seim.

Then I got to thinking about when Ben, just for the hell of it, roped a bobcat. He took a double half-hitch with the rope around the horn, so he could shoot the cat, but he hadn't caught it around the neck but around the middle. He didn't have time to shoot it before the bobcat came up the rope flying and jumped on the back of Ben's horse. That horse turned to bucking in a hurry and Ben came off pretty fast. I wasn't sure if the horse threw him or if he just decided he didn't like riding double with a bobcat. Anyway, Ben landed on the ground and the bobcat flew off the horse too. The bobcat wedged himself under a pile of logs, and that horse jerked on the rope a bit harder than that cat could take, killing the bobcat and breaking the rope about the same time. I had to run down Ben's horse and bring him back. That horse sure was rope shy after that. Dad had managed to trade him to a homesteader who couldn't rope, so they got along fine.

Another time, Ben and I had been out giving a couple of green horses a long ride, and when we got back to camp late in the afternoon, we headed for the house to call it a day. We were more than a little surprised to see a cow's head sticking out of the door of the house. The door wasn't open far enough for her to get all the way back out, but she sure was trying to get out. One of us must have left the door a little open when we left in the morning. I might have been the last one out of the house as I was in an awful hurry to get out to the outhouse. From there I went straight to the corral and we went riding.

"Bob, why'd you leave that door open?" Ben accused me somewhat flabbergasted.

I tried to lay some foundation for doubt. "I'm sure I shut the door, but maybe someone like Brave Bear, or one of them L-C cowboys stopped by while we were gone." I suspected that I was the guilty one, but more importantly, I wondered how we would get that cow out of the house without getting stomped on.

She wasn't one of our Durham cows. She was yellow and white spotted with a white triangle on the front of her face. As soon as Ben saddled a fresh horse and gathered up his rope, he said to me,

"When my rope lands around her neck, take a pole and shove the door open." I expected that cow to come unglued when that rope tightened on her neck, but she just walked out like a halter-broke horse. Ben said, "Looks like someone had broken that cow to lead— she's just like an old pet." Ben led her out some ways from the house and turned her loose, and we went about cleaning up a messed up house. If you can imagine what a cow can do in a few hours inside of a house, she had done it all and didn't miss a thing. It took some doing to get it some cleaned up. The place still smelled like a cow barn most of the winter.

Next morning that Guernsey heifer was lying right outside the door and followed us out to the corral, so we just let her in with the horses. She didn't have a brand or mark of any kind on her, and we had no idea where she came from. But we figured that she likely came from over west across the county line, where they had opened up Perkins County for homesteading in the spring of 1907. She likely got away from one of the homesteaders. They had to have a shack on their claim and live on it for three years, and they had to have a cow, or critters of some sort, and a plow in order to get clear title to the land. Ben came up with the idea that if someone didn't come by and claim old Guernsey by the time we run another bunch of cattle up to Thunder Hawk, we would just take her along for Abe and Jim to milk. We knew she was some kind of a milk cow and was looking like she was already making bag. No one came for our milk cow. We gathered in a few calves that we missed on the first gather and the Guernsey really made herself to home. It was getting into hard winter in January, and we wanted to get rid of our cattle chores at the camp. But we got a few warm days, so I just chased the calves and that Guernsey heifer up to Thunder Hawk, while Ben took care of watering and checking our cows on Thunder Hawk Creek.

When we were leaving, I happened to notice that Guernsey cow was in the corral and mentioned to Jim that cow had to be getting old. She would have been coming up on fourteen and that is really old for a range cow. Well that really opened up the floodgates. Jim went on and on about that cow, "Damned old cow, she would have died a long time ago if I had anything to do with her life span.

Mother thinks the world of that cow, but she is the most cantankerous critter I've ever seen. Makes me want to get away from home just so I don't have to contend with that old bitty. If you leave a door or a gate a little open, she can make it through it in a flash. You can't sit a feed bucket down without her having her head in it. If she can get close to you, she licks you, and she likes to lick you when you are milking her. She has the about roughest tongue, like getting a coarse sandpaper rub, only a lot wetter!"

"I guess you rather not have cream in your coffee or fresh butter every day," answered Mother. She liked the milk and cream that cow produced, and she wasn't about to let Jim's complaining change that. That Guernsey cow stayed on for several more years.

Morning came about at its usual time, but we were up early and ready to hunt for cattle. Where to hunt was the question. We decided to ride west and check with our neighbor Herb Lyman who had picked up my homestead quarter. He was running quite a few cattle, so if there were any of Ben's around, he likely would know of their whereabouts. Riding west, we saw a lot of changes. The first I noticed was a school house, just a little over a half a mile from our camp. A family named Montgomery had bought Dad's homestead, and they had put up a wooden windmill, built a barn, and housed chickens in Dad's old cabin. They made a house by digging into the side of an old bank: it had a roof over it with a big window and a door next to it on the south side. We hadn't figured on stopping, but Carl Montgomery was out by the well; so we swung our horses over in his direction just to say hello.

He was happy to see us and insisted that we come in. "Meet the family," he said and waved his arm at what was a good-sized family to meet. He had only one wife, but there were more than six kids with the oldest one only looking maybe thirteen. We had a cup of coffee, and after an hour or so of listening to all the gossip in the Grand Valley, we bid our good-byes and were back on our horses going on a fast pace in the direction of Herb Lyman's headquarters.

Herb was out in the corral working with a young horse when we rode into the yard, so we just rode over to the corral. Before we could get off our horses and tie them to the corral, Herb was standing in front of us with a pleasant look about him. He greeted me with "Thank God, you made it back. I knew you went off to war but never heard if you survived it or not. Good to see you again." We shook hands, then he shook Jim's hand. "You are sure growing up to be long stream of water," he said sizing up Jim. "Come on over to the house. It's time for a spot of tea!" His wife Helen met us at the door, and I got a quick hug and a friendly greeting. Herb had it figured out already that we were looking for cattle or horses, and he just happened to know where there were a few of ours. We were soon seated at the kitchen table with a cup of hot tea in front of us. We had a lot to talk about, mostly small talk. Lunchtime came and we were still into swapping stories. Gathering cattle could wait another day.

Herb had some other land further over to the west. It was pretty much open range from the Grand River on over west clear to Seim except for the homesteaders who had fenced their land. Mostly what was left for cattle to run at large in were the rough brakes that no one wanted. Herb and George Minges were running cattle in common together on that land. There had been some of Ben's cows and a couple of Dad's B-bar-B branded cows over there, too, and they had been there for a while. A little band of horses was running over there as well. No one was claiming them, but Herb was sure some of them were our horses. "Why don't you wait until we have started our roundup in a couple of months and ride over with us and gather up the cattle? George and I are going to need some extra help. You could sort the cows and hold them over at George's place, which is only about five miles southwest of here. Then we could all work together and get all of the cattle branded," he offered.

I agreed, "Sounds to me like it would be the easiest way to gather that bunch of cows."

Herb went on to say, "There're half a dozen of Ben's cows over south too, just a little east of the old Duncan place."

I knew that area well, so I said, "Herb, I think that we could ride out to that area in the afternoon and be back in time to go with you for the roundup."

"Good. Be here the last day of October—that's when we plan to gather in our cattle," said Herb with a grin. Helen put a big meal on the table right at noon, and we left their house pretty full as we headed south.

It didn't take long before we came up on some cattle along West Cottonwood Creek. None of them were ours, so we rode on by without even disturbing them. We went on over to the big spring, but no cattle. Then we made a swing over to the reservation line just east of the hogback where we jumped up a few cows that headed east on a run. They all had Ben's brand on them. By the time we got caught up to them, they had picked up some more cows, and we had a dozen head with five of them having Dad's brand, but none of their calves were branded. We headed them for camp—it was four miles back to camp and we never seen another cow along the way. We did see a lot the Duncan's sheep, but we didn't have time to stop and talk. We figured we could catch up with them on another day knowing that people with sheep were never far from their flock. We made it back to camp before dark, but not in time to do any branding, so that would be our first priority job in the morning. Dad had said that all us boys, including Abe, could split between us all Ben's cattle that we got gathered in. It was crossing my mind that maybe Abe should be there helping too.

CHAPTER 9

Old Horses

Jim was a good hand, and we managed to get the cattle brand-ed, but it was a hot August day, and we didn't do any castrations or dehorning. Past experiences had taught us not to because in hot weather, maggots tend to infest any open wounds and cause so much infection that if not treated, the critter could die. Since our camp at the river was really overrun with mosquitoes, we decided to head the cattle up to Thunder Hawk and maybe take a run over west of Herb Lyman's place to see if we could catch up with that little band of wild horses. Abe, once again, didn't make his pres-ence known, but Jim was up early and had a couple of fresh horses caught up for our ride. It was going to be another hot day, but there was a strong north breeze that would help if we managed to find any horses. Horses, cows too, like to go into the wind on a hot day. We headed south by southwest with Jim doing the guiding. He knew all of the back trails around or through the homesteads. In ten years' time, the whole area had taken on a complete change. There were people living on every quarter of land between Thunder Hawk and the Grand River, and Jim knew them all. Some he had words with so he said. Keeping it to myself, I wondered what kind of words?

I was feeling the need of a coffee break when we were coming up on Andy Pearson's place. I suggested, well insisted, to Jim that we stop by and see if Slim was back yet and let our horses catch their wind. Andy was out in the yard chopping wood and right away came over and persuaded us to light down and come in. It didn't take long to be in the house with a cup of java in front of us. After some small talk, I asked, "Have you seen anything of that Slim Summers? He couldn't wait to get home to your daughter Alma when we were doing our errand for Uncle Sam."

Andy said with a big smile, "Sure have. He's been back for most neigh a month now. He took on a job spike pitching for a thrashing crew over at Thumb Kittleson's place, three or so miles south of Thunder Hawk. Alma went along to help with the cooking. Slim and Alma haven't been apart much since he got home. They are planning to get married very shortly."

We were soon back in the saddle and looking for wild horses. It was getting close to midday, and we were in the area where Herb said that the horses had been grazing. There were fresh horse tracks but no horses in sight. There were a few scattered homesteaders south of the river, but a lot of the land was too rough or too poor for homesteaders to have any desire for it, so it was a good area for anything wild. As we were riding along south of the river a few miles, Jim pointed to a lone homesteader's shack along the south slope of a high hill and said, "Let's just ask that homesteader if he's seen any horses around lately?" I agreed, and we rode up toward the shack. He wasn't such a big fellow, but about the time we were a hundred feet from his house, he met us with a shotgun pointed right at us. That made him look mighty big.

"If you fellows are looking for trouble, you've come to the right place," he said before either of us could speak.

I looked him right in the eye and said, "Friend, that's the last thing we're looking for. We think we have some horses running around in these parts and just came by looking to find them."

He lowered his shotgun and said, "In that case, I can tell you where your horses are. They have been a damned nuisance ever since I've been here. Just ride on over west about two miles—they were over just north of Dane Anderson's place yesterday."

"Much obliged," I answered, and we turned and headed west a bit faster than we had ridden in. I had no idea who or where Dane Anderson's place was, but Jim knew him and said that Dane was a great fellow who wouldn't run us off with a shotgun. Didn't take us long to make it over west a couple of miles, but it was more like three or four miles to Dane's place. He greeted us and insisted that we come in for lunch. Dane and his wife, Matilda, didn't have a lot, but most homesteaders were in that boat. They had a couple of young boys with patches on their pants. Matilda, who was in the family way again, soon had a plate of hot food in front of us. It sure tasted good after the long stretch since breakfast. Dane knew exactly where our horses were. Said he had seen my R hanging G brand on a couple of the old mares.

The horses were in a draw drinking water from a spring less than a quarter of a mile from the Anderson homestead. They weren't wild, and I did recognize the old mares in particular. I had driven them some as a team—Dad had traded them off to someone heading west who needed a fresh team. The mares must have ran away, came back as far as they could get to home, and started raising colts. I said to my little brother, "Those mares got bred somewhere along the way, like as not before they made their escape. When the oldest stud colt got old enough to breed, he likely serviced the old mares." We were looking at thirteen horses in all with two suckling colts. That was enough to give us a job breaking horses for the next month or so.

I spoke as soft as I could to Jim, "Ride around to the far side of the horses, and try roping one of the old mares. I will pull down my rope too. Whichever one of us gets a chance first should rope one of them. It'll be a lot easier to lead one than trying to chase them out of this rough terrain." Jim rode right up to one of the old mares and had her snagged before I even got a chance to dally my rope. Once caught, the mare led like an old broke horse. Jim headed on toward home, and I hazed the other horses along, but they mostly wanted to follow the old mare anyway.

Dane had said that the fellow with the shotgun went by the name of Albert Wood, and Albert had a still hid somewhere on his place so that was why he gave us such a friendly welcome. We didn't swing by his place on the way home, but with the whole country going dry, it might come in handy knowing where we could find some hooch. Indians couldn't drink anyway by law, but making it a law only made people want to drink. With these new Prohibition laws, the whites couldn't drink either, so I reckoned they would want to drink now even if they never drank before.

Dad recognized the team of mares right off and said he had traded them to a homesteader up around Pretty Rock country some twenty miles north of Thunder Hawk. He said that fellow, Bill Mathenay, came back a dozen times looking for his horses. He accused about everyone and his brother of stealing his team. "So, Jim, my boy," he said, "you can take his horses back and explain where you found them. Bob, you can start tomorrow at breaking that string of rough stock you just brought in," adding, "We'll see if you can still sit astride a wild bronco."

Breaking broncos was a hard and busy kind of work. Jim could ride most any horse, and he liked doing it. I liked letting him, so that part worked well for both of us. There is more to breaking broncos, though, than riding them for ten seconds. It takes miles of riding and working a horse to teach it to be trustworthy enough so anyone can hop on without having a wreck. We managed after a month to get half a dozen horses trained to ride, and Dad, with his skills as a horse trader, managed to sell them for us.

October was on us, and it was time to start looking for the cattle. Herb Lyman was expecting us when we rode in to help with his roundup. The weather had caught cold again, and it started raining before we arrived at Lyman's. As we were putting our horses up for the night, it turned to a wet snow. Herb wasn't one to call off a roundup because of weather and said, "This snow will make it easier to gather the cattle. They'll bunch up and head for home, or at least be looking for feed and shelter." After three days of looking, finding, and sorting cattle, we did find three pairs of Ben's cows and trailed them back to Thunder Hawk. We had found ten of Ben's cows total, so we did a three-way split, and the extra cow went to

Dad for pasture rent on the others. I was back in the cow business again, but it didn't take a genius to figure out that I didn't have enough cattle to make a living. I'd have to find some other way to support myself.

CHAPTER 10

Far from Wisconsin

Dad had gotten to know Walter Fero right when the family got off the boxcar at the Thunder Hawk siding. Like a lot of Dakota homesteaders, Walter and Martha Fero were leaving an old life as much as coming to a new one. Most everybody wondered why they had left behind such a comfortable and prosperous life, but nobody asked. That wasn't done. Walter talked about the cheese factory in Muscoda, Wisconsin, that he'd run with nearly thirty farmers supplying milk for his prize-winning cheese. Dad, though, had this kind of open way about him, and people often told him things they wouldn't talk about with anybody else. I guess pretty much everybody knew Dad's story, so it was all right to tell something of theirs. Here's how I remember Dad telling me about the Feros and how our families became so wound together.

In 1899, when little Charlie was not yet known as "Tubby," Walter had won the first prize gold medal at a cheese-making contest in Chicago. Walter carried around a wrinkled newspaper, the *New York Produce Review*, that had a photo of him and Martha with young Charlie and Dwight dressed up in the kinda "dress" that young city boys still wore then until they were about five. Walter was quoted in that newspaper saying, "My wife and children are not by any means silent partners in the factory; I can make better cheese while thinking of my babies, and what should I not do for her who left her home and friends in faraway Canada to be by my side."

I'd guess that Walter probably had no idea when his boys were still wearing those dresses how those words would come to haunt his life. But maybe he just wasn't cut out for the solid but dull life of making cheese. He told how his French ancestors had come to the New World in the 1600s and maybe that wanderlust just carried Walter and his family down on to the northern plains. By 1902, ambition and hard work had gotten Walter and Martha their own cheese factory in Stanley, Wisconsin, and by 1906, they sold the factory and land for a profit and were thinking about what to do next. Walter had invested some of the profits in fancy horses, including a stepping horse and a blooded race horse. Then tragedy struck.

Schoolboys Charlie and Dwight were hurrying back home after a late fall afternoon spent hunting in the nearby woods with the new shotgun Charlie had gotten for his fourteenth birthday. Charlie was carrying the single-barrel hammer shotgun across his arm pointed toward his friend Leslie walking at his side.

"Charlie, have you got any more of that chewing gum?" asked Leslie.

Charlie reached his arm back to put his hand in his pocket, and his sleeve caught on the hammer. The gun went off, instantly killing his best friend. The local paper summed up the tragedy in its headline: "Another young life was sacrificed to the 'Boy and Gun' fad here last Saturday."

No one in the town directly blamed Charlie, but the stares and the faces that turned away from the family were more than they could bear. It was especially hard for Martha, who had lost a baby girl to enteritis not so many years before. Walter wanted to move on and leave that awful death behind them, so they did. He had been reading the Wisconsin newspaper accounts of homestead land for the taking on the Standing Rock Reservation in South Dakota since the land had opened up to white settlement. He liked the idea of striking out for what the railroads were advertising as the "last frontier."

"By God," he said, "we won't stay here where a man can't look you in the eye."

"Do you think we'll ever get away from Leslie's shade?" asked Martha.

"Charlie deserves a new start, and we all need to wake up without seeing those damned woods. There is land for free or for cheap out west. Just look at what the railroads say about this new homestead land in South Dakota."

Martha knew without looking that it was time to start sorting and packing. She had followed Walter to Wisconsin and now she would follow him to South Dakota, and she would do her best to remake the world she had known for her family there. So she gathered up flower seeds and rose cuttings to plant and tend in different soil. In April, they sold all the Wisconsin property, loaded up a boxcar with a wagon, some farming tools, a milk cow, the blooded racehorse, and the family's furniture and household goods, and headed west. When their boxcar pulled off at the siding in Thunder Hawk, Jim Hourigan and Dad met them at the Thunder Hawk station and acted as locaters—that is local land promoters—and helped the family find a homestead. Most of the land had been taken up by then, but some homesteaders had already left failing to prove up their claims, and Dad showed him how to take advantage. Walter filed for 320 acres about two miles east of Thunder Hawk, advertised that his racehorse, *Macresse*, would be standing at stud every Friday and Saturday, and set about building a large Wisconsin-style dairy barn.

Charlie and Dwight took to the cowboy life like ducks to water. They roamed the land from Pumpkin Butte to Black Horse Butte on horseback with Jimmy, Abe, and the other boys learning how to herd cattle and set up a camp in the cottonwoods. Some said the Fero boys were a little wild, but Walter let them have their way and their fast horses. They made it through the eighth grade at Thunder Hawk's room school, but that was all the education that either ever managed much to Martha's disappointment. Their new life was full, and no one ever asked Walter why they came to

Dakota. No one ever knew about Charlie's night terrors. Everyone else held their reasons close for coming to the Dakotas, and they didn't need to share them.

If Walter looked back to Wisconsin, it wasn't more than a quick glance. And cheese making would not be his life's work. He turned out to be not so much of a farmer as he was a land and horse trader. He and Martha tried a variety of businesses, including a hotel, but settled on a flour and feed store, which they did well with before things went bust. Walter traded a team of horses to a failed homesteader for a piano for Martha to play and entertain their family, which soon included two little girls.

Our families were near neighbors by Dakota standards—only a couple of miles—and we spent time socializing together. Charlie had heard talk about Bob's younger sister Bessie who was away at Carlisle Indian College. Bessie had been away for most of four years when she stepped off the train wearing a dark blue, traveling suit and a picture-book hat.

"My God, girl, you're a sight for sore eyes," Dad said, his voice somewhere between a whisper and a shout.

"*Cunksi, Ake iyuskinyan wancinyankelo* (Daughter, I am glad to see you again)," said her mother. I gave her big hug and swung her around the platform. Jim didn't quite know what to say, so he just hugged her and swung her around too. Abe and Viola showed off their baby girl to her Aunt Bess.

"It's good to be home," Bess said, taking in all the open space around her from the station platform. "Home is where you can see all the sky. You wouldn't believe how many trees there are in Pennsylvania—it's all trees if it's not towns and cornfields. I've left many friends at school," she said with what looked like a little mist in her eye, "but here is where I will stay. At school, they taught us that we must make the most of our 'advantages.' I will try to do that. Mother, I am so hungry. Are we going home to dinner?"

"Yes, we will go home, and our neighbors will be joining us for a picnic under the cottonwood trees. They have grown taller as you have while you were away," Mother replied.

Standing near our family, the Fero brothers and sisters looked on in wonder. Little Eve reached up to touch the fluffy feather on Bess's hat.

Martha welcomed her by saying, "Now, we have another musician. We can play piano duets. And I won't have to be the only one playing for socials at the schoolhouse."

Bessie was introduced all around, and we all piled into buggies and wagons and headed to the picnic under the cottonwood trees. Charlie was wearing his best rodeo dude outfit with chaps, cuffs, and a nice, new gray Stetson. In five years, he had never seen a woman like Bessie, and he was smitten right then and there. After the apple pie and the chocolate cake were served, Dad played fiddle and everybody danced out on the grass until it was too dark to see anymore. That picnic under the trees was one of the best anyone remembered.

Charlie wasn't much like the boys Bess had known at college, but he sure knew how to dance and how to pay compliments to a young woman. He could make her forget another dashing man in a letterman's sweater back at Carlisle who was too busy with football games and running around a track to have a place in his life for a woman like Bess. At Carlisle, the students rooted for the "Indians" against their main rivals, the fighting "Irish" of Notre Dame. Bessie wondered about the names of some of the other teams, like "Tigers," but she understood that like the Indians, the Irish were outsiders trying to prove themselves, or prove something to themselves. She had admired that fellow's skill on the football field as she cheered for her school, and she'd heard the talk that he would run in Olympics in Europe soon, but nothing was ever said. They took long walks on campus, but nothing was ever promised. When she got back home, Bess worked hard to help her mother at home, and by fall she had put her photos of her Carlisle classmates, including the special one of the dark-haired man with a big *C* for Carlisle on his football uniform sweater, in the bottom of her traveling trunk. She kept herself busy organizing a lending library for Thunder Hawk, substituting for some of school teachers, and giving piano lessons.

Dad played fiddle for the dancing at Charlie and Bess's wedding in October. Martha cut the last flowers from her garden for Bess to carry and played the piano for the ceremony. Bess wore the white lawn dress with pin tucks all down the front that she made as her graduation outfit for Carlisle. Just about everybody around came to the Presbyterian Church in Thunder Hawk. When the big spread with a beef barbeque put on at the schoolhouse and the dancing was over, Bess and Charlie motored over to Bess's quarter section of land in Charlie's new Model T Ford. A two-room frame house had already been put up about a mile from our homeplace, but there were many more buildings needed to get their farm ready. Like so many others, they were eager to plough and plant the prairie soil to make money on the high wheat prices that had come with the end of the Great War. They would raise wheat and a few head of cattle there—it was good land that had never been turned over by a plough. Charlie didn't know much about farming, but he did know all about the new farm tractors and machinery, and he figured that he and Bess would have one of the best farms around.

The Deadwood Trail

Bess and Tubby's wedding had been about the best party in those parts until Slim and Alma tied the knot, and Andy Pearson gave them a wedding dance in the loft of his barn. Everyone from miles around came. Dad volunteered his services as fiddle player and joined up with Jon Wiesinger who played an accordion and his cousin, Jake Wiesinger, who picked a guitar. The Wiesinger homestead was twenty miles south of Lemmon, but they played for dances far and wide. I got beckoned, front and center by my friend Slim, to call a few squares, but I was a tad rusty at that calling bit. It had been a long while since I had called a square dance. Slim and I had went to a dance back before army days, and I had called at that dance. A lot of water had gone under the bridge since then, but I still called well enough to have the dancers swinging high. When the musicians took a break, Abe whispered at me, "Come on out with me. I have something that will help with your calling."

Prohibition was in full force throughout the country, but Abe and a good share of the gents outside had a jug of moonshine. Tubby Fero was among the crowd outside the barn. He handed me a jug and said, "Made it myself. Me and my brother Dwight and Todd Kruze have a little still. Why don't you partner with us and help us distribute our product?" Tubby had become a bootlegger on the side and was making more moonshine than the local boys could drink. Like a lot of people at that time, he saw a way to make some money without too much effort. Tubby, being married, and to my sister, couldn't be away from home for long, and they needed someone to haul their hooch to other towns, someone they could trust to avoid getting caught, but not squealing on them if he was caught. Tubby knew I wouldn't squeal, plus I had driven an ambulance in the army, so I could drive a car fast. Tubby had a way of making friends; he was easy to like and just a peach of a fellow. He was by far my best brother-in-law. Bessie didn't drink and didn't think much of people who did, but she loved Tubby and made herself look the other way and not at the moonshine operation.

Times had become very hard for wheat farmers like Tubby. After the war, the boom in grain prices went bust leaving them with grain prices that were sinking like a stone in a well. Then one Friday, the Bank of Thunder Hawk just closed its doors and never opened them again. Lots of people lost everything they had, including my dad and Tubby's folks. It didn't take much for a small town bank to fail in those days: one year of bad crops for farmers or a hard winter for ranchers could do it. There had been runs on banks all over North Dakota and South Dakota with people demanding their money. Old Harold Jorgenson, the bank president, who had been one of the biggest boosters of Thunder Hawk, just hustled himself out of town on the train going east and left nothing behind, not even an explanation. There wasn't any run on the bank, just that big hand-lettered "Closed" sign. Dad, the old Scotchman that he was, had a good-sized nest egg in the bank too. We had wholeheartedly trusted the bank. Everyone with money in the bank just lost it. Some other banks that closed that year reopened, but a lot of money was lost to the banks.

Dad liked to play cards with the boys at the pool hall in Thunder Hawk, and he wasn't above having a few shots of whiskey either, but after losing all of his money it seemed to set him off to drinking on a regular basis. The difference now was that he didn't have extra money to spend on booze. He just kind of gave up and didn't seem to care what was happening on the homeplace. Mother talked to him about his drinking to no avail. He should have buried some of his nest egg or kept it in a tobacco can, some did, and they had money, but mostly people were broke. I guess we all should have, but hindsight is always twenty-twenty. Now I had to find a way to make a new start, and Tubby's offer looked pretty good.

Tubby had three little girls to feed and take care of. Bessie had been cutting up her fancy dresses from her college days back east to make clothes for them. Nobody had money for piano lessons after the bank closed. Like some of the other farmers, Tubby had just shot some of his cows rather than try to get them to market. So after a lot of rumination, Tubby had all the details worked out for his operation. He even had a car; it was an Overland Roadster. The roadster was top of the line for fast cars and had plenty of room for crates of hooch in its trunk. This moonshine operation had the making of a lucrative way to make money, and it was a far cry easier than busting broncos for a living. Besides, the horse market was looking like a thing of the past, with cars and trains fast replacing horses for transportation and steam engines and big machines replacing work horses. Getting caught could be a problem—with the new federal Prohibition law, the threat of another jail sentence could be discouraging. With Prohibition came the lawmen to enforce it. Prohibition officers were running around the area like chickens with their heads chopped off. Revenuers were easy to spot with their fancy city clothes and new cars. However, the real giveaway was the barrage of questions they threw at any and about all they encountered. The rabbit has to be smarter than the fox in order to survive, and there are a lot more rabbits than foxes. I thought, "I might just be a rabbit."

Stills were cropping up all over with the federal agents finding quite a few of them. One of their finds was a still in a root cellar. A few of the stills were made with some degree of intelligence, but many were just cobbled up affairs and the hooch from them was questionable at best. Our still had a copper boiler, and it got cleaned thoroughly after each use. We used glass coils for the hooch to run out of, but some used copper tubing and if not cleaned, it would produce a toxic poisoning in the hooch. Tubby was no dummy—he hid our still in a well. He and his brother Dwight had dug a well on Tubby and Bessie's homestead a few miles to the south of Thunder Hawk. Then down in the well ten feet, they dug out a room to the side of the well. The well was just outside of a shed that was their workshop with a stove and a forge for blacksmithing. They ran a brick chimney from the ground up for the stove in the shop. Unknown to most, the chimney from the still stove fit into the bottom of the brick chimney. The boys had dug the well down over twenty feet but hadn't hit water; so if someone came snooping around, the boys could just be digging on the well. You had to dig deep to hit water on the plains. Also they planked the walls of the well to keep it from caving in on them, and one of the planks was a trick door to their still. You had to jiggle a certain spot on one of the boards just right for the door to open. Then to cover any smell and maybe, toy with the revenuers, Tubby and his brother built a smokehouse by the shed and smoked hams and such while they were cooking up a batch of hooch.

Todd Kruze knew a lot of people who were wanting to buy some booze, so he went with me for my first run. We loaded up the roadster with hooch and headed south. Tubby cautioned us saying, "Most bootleggers are caught in the small towns. It's best to avoid places like Isabel and Faith and head straight to Deadwood and then on over to Rapid City."

Todd knew the people and places to deliver to, so our run went without attracting any federal agents, but he didn't want to hang around Deadwood. He told about when he stayed there one other time and it didn't turn out the best. "I made my delivery and it was getting late, so I got a room at the Franklin Hotel. I wanted a hot meal and maybe a drink, so I went across the street to the Old Style Number 10 Saloon," he related. Deadwood was a thriving mining town nestled in a valley with hills covered with pine trees. It had grown in size since Brave Bear and I were there a dozen years ago. He continued, "The bars in Deadwood don't pay much heed to the Prohibition law. It would be easier to rope a bobcat by the tail than stop a bunch of miners from drinking. Maybe the miners went on strike for booze, but more likely the miners put the fear of meeting God into the revenuers. Anyway, for some reason, Deadwood isn't quite a dry town."

Todd went on to tell me about his night in Deadwood. "The saloon had some musicians playing, and it was crowded with people there for the dancing. I had just grabbed a drink and some dinner and was thinking about heading back to my room. Then this good-looking gal comes waltzing over, just friendlier than a speckled pup. I bought her a drink, and she told me her name was Pie. After a few dances, she whispered in my ear, 'Want to go someplace and have a piece of Pie?' I liked pie, so we went straight to my room, and I was about to try a sample of pie when the door came flying open.

"Pouncing through the door was her husband, Al, looking mad, mean, and in a mood to fight, saying, 'Nobody dinks my wife. I'll knock you from here to breakfast.'

" 'She wasn't wearing no ring,' I sputtered. I looked at her, but she didn't deny she was Al's wife. Then Al made a dive for me. I stepped aside and he landed belly down on the floor. Before he could regain his upright posture, I grabbed up my clothes and ran to my car and lit out for Rapid City. That's why I don't spend a lot of time in Deadwood."

I didn't comment on the subject, but my thoughts were "better him than me."

It was soon evident that we couldn't keep up with the demand for our product with just our one still. Consequently, we started looking elsewhere for more spirit waters. Canada was the closest place; it was legal to buy good whiskey there, and the border patrol was easy enough to bypass if you knew the area. There were plenty of back trails that the border patrol didn't watch much at night. I had made several runs to Canada where whiskey was relatively cheap, and it sold for sometimes ten times what we paid for it; so it made for a profitable business.

One late night, I hadn't seen another soul on the dusty back road out of Manitoba. I was pushing the roadster at high speed when I came over a little hill and up front of me in the headlights I could see a wall of woolies laying on the road. I was going too fast to stop, so I just stepped on the gas, thinking I might make it over that flock of sheep. I did wobble and weave over a lot of them, but about the time I could see clear road ahead, the roadster came to a stop with several sheep wedged under it. I thought about my plight for a second; if I waited for the owner of the sheep and pay him for the dead sheep, there would be a lot of questions about why I was traveling on this back road. My whiskey-running days might end. I bailed out, jacked up the roadster, and started pulling sheep out from under it. Sure it hadn't done the sheep much good; they were all dead. I was just pulling the last sheep out from under the roadster when I saw a lantern coming down the hill behind me. Most likely it was the sheepherder. He was hollering something that didn't sound friendly that might have been in French as they do speak a lot of French in Canada. I didn't wait to find out what he had hollered, just jumped back under the wheel, jerked the roadster into gear, hitting the throttle hard, and went speeding on my way. I heard one shot, but that fellow must have been too far away or a poor shot. I didn't feel anything hit the roadster or me, so I got out of that one with only memories. I never took that particular road again. Trails like that one were better left alone, like a sleeping dog.

Bootlegging and rum running became big business in North Dakota during those days when ranchers and farmers could hardly make ends meet, and it sure kept a lot of Prohibition agents in jobs. The bulk of the newcomers were homesteaders as poor as church mice, and mostly they were an honest and hardworking lot, but farming was not making most of them enough money to live on; so some were turning to moonshining like Tubby. Many of these folks had come from Europe, where having a beer or a shot of whiskey was part of their way of life. Indians never had booze of any kind before the white man introduced them to it and had no tolerance to alcohol. They got drunk easy and it brought out the worst in them, but when the law said they couldn't drink, like the whites, it only made them want to drink. Homemade beer and wine became popular as did the moonshine.

I had dropped off a delivery in Dickenson one particular day and didn't have any whiskey with me. I got a few miles south of Dickenson when I saw the road was blocked up ahead and spied a string of revenuers' cars in the rear view mirror. Those boys really meant business, so I just stopped. I was jerked out of the roadster and cuffed in nothing flat. They about tore the roadster apart, but they couldn't find a thing.

The one in charge, who called himself "Two-Gun" Hart, was all duded up in a ten-gallon hat and chaps. He wore a pistol on his left hip and had a rifle hanging over his right arm. Two-Gun finally came over to me, taking the cuffs off, and said, "Maybe I was ill-informed, but you'd better be dang sure that I am watchin' you. You breeds just better stay outta the hooch business."

Those revenuers paid informants a little cash, so I suppose one of the lads around Thunder Hawk had turned me in for a few bucks or the devil of it. Two-Gun had been making quite a name for himself. He had been a hero as a sharpshooter in France during the war, and it was said he could shoot a bottle out of the air before you could even see him raise his gun. He had been hired by the Bureau of Indian Affairs as a Prohibition officer to stop whiskey on reservations. However, Dickenson was a long way from his stomping grounds, so he must have been trailing this particular Indian. He had been catching bootleggers and busting up stills all across South Dakota and Nebraska, but I hadn't heard of him being in North Dakota before. Besides, part of the Standing Rock Reservation, the lands of the Three Affiliated Tribes, and Turtle Mountain Reservation were in North Dakota, so he had a lot of territory to cover. For every still that was found, two weren't found, so bootlegging was flourishing in spite of the revenuers.

This Two-Gun had bragged around that he was some kind of Nebraska Indian, but he was a little vague on just what tribe and didn't look like any of the Indians I knew. Some said he was a Mexican or maybe Apache. So I said polite like in Lakota, "Who are you? Where are you from? *(Nituwe hwo? Nituktetanhan hwo?)*"

He just gave me long stare and said again, "I'll be watchin' you."

I didn't try to make enemies, but there were those who just didn't like me. Jealousy was some of their motive, but a dislike for Indians ran deep with some too. About every time I attended a social function, some fellow or two would try to get a fight out of me or one of my brothers, and we mostly were obliging. Jim was always getting into a fight; he usually would win but came out of the fight looking in worse shape than the fellow that lost the fight. Jim was fond of saying that it's not the size of the man in the fight but the size of the fight in the man that counts. He could be right. At any rate, he always had a lot of fight in him.

Jim and I went to a dance at the Town Hall in Thunder Hawk that August. People seem to always have time for a dance or party even when they're dead broke, and this dance was no exception— there was a large crowd of people. The musicians had taken a break, so some of us boys went outside to have a little nip. It was a nice, moonlit, summer night, and no revenuers around. We had passed the bottle around to our little group of friends—Earl Williamson, Ernie and Levi Wagner, the three Hourigan brothers, Ben Irons, Henry Ploog, Ace Kempton, with Jim and Abe rounding out our group. Another group of fellows came out of the dance hall and kind of formed a circle around us.

"You damn breeds either leave right now or we are going to kick your asses," bellowed out one big guy in that group.

Well, that was just too much for Earl. "I just came back from fighting a war and some of these breeds fighting at my side in that war happen to be the reason I made it back alive. You yellow-bellied, draft dodgers have been bullying long enough." And he let fly, hitting that fellow square with a haymaker, sitting him on the ground. That brought out the desire to fight in the boys around us and then everyone went to swinging. We were outnumbered some, but we had more experience. The fight ended with Earl and his breeds going back into the dance hall with the fight knocked out of the tough-talking fellows.

My brother Ben had been sweet on Earl's older sister Maude back a few years. She hadn't come to the dance, but his younger sisters as well as some younger brothers were with him. Altogether there were fourteen Williamsons. One of Earl's younger sisters, Elizabeth Jane—she preferred being called Betty—caught my attention. She could sure dance and was quite good to look at too. Her short dress printed with blue flowers seemed to float around her, and it showed off her trim figure and bright blue eyes. She was on the quiet side and didn't drink. After a few waltzes around the floor, I said, "I haven't seen you too much before. I guess you like to dance. You sure are a good dancer."

"Earl has told me some about you. Besides fighting in the war, I know that you were down at Leavenworth for shooting a man. He said you didn't do it. Compared to that, my life is pretty tame. Mostly I stay home and help my folks take care of the younger kids."

"Could I see you home after the dance?" I asked.

"Sure," she said, "but I have a boyfriend. John Ellison was supposed to take me to this dance, but he didn't show up. I have been seeing him for quite a while now."

I liked her a lot, but she talked about John Ellison most of the way home. She was hoping he would ask her to marry in the near future. I left her thinking that John might have other plans, and so did I.

CHAPTER 12

Hauling Double Barrels

Times were changing for Indians but only very slowly. The government had voted to accept all Indians as citizens in 1924. I had my citizenship paper given to me because I fought for this country and with my honorable discharge came my citizenship. Indians who served in the Great War were given citizenship in 1919, but all the other Indians were still just considered to be wards of the government who'd be better off if they gave up their "Indianness" and assimilated. The Mormons contended that the Indians were the Lost Tribe of Israel, so they treated the Indians kindly and made friends with them wherever they traveled. At least they looked at Indians as a people. There were some whose main motive was greed for Indian lands. Some had said Indians derived from the monkey family and weren't even people, so annihilating the Indian was in the same category as ending a species from the animal kingdom. The churches still ran the schools and hospitals on the reservations. On the other hand, many people tried to get a better deal for the Indians after the war. Some back east even thought Indian veterans should have the same benefits as white veterans. After the war, some politicians paid attention to some of the wrongs that happened to the Indians and tried to set things right. There were parades and ceremonies, but very little money flowed toward the reservations.

Some on Standing Rock tried to keep up the old ways, and some embraced the changes knowing that the old ways were gone after Wounded Knee. Some tried to get ahead through getting an education, some tried to build up bigger ranches, and some like me found ways to make a living out of the changes, including Prohibition. I devised several different ways to run alcohol down from Canada. With the North Dakota border getting hard to slip across, I started making my runs by way of Montana or Minnesota. The North Dakota State Police had been arming themselves with machine guns and stepped up boarder enforcement by several notches. It took a lot longer to make a run, and we couldn't keep up with the demand for our product.

Tubby came up with another plan. He was good at planning things to the last detail, and he mostly had good plans. Guess that would make him the brains behind the operation. He knew a fellow who knew another fellow who could get us a lot of whiskey, but we would have to drive a truck over east to Chicago. I was the elected driver, and the disguise was to make it look like we were hauling gasoline. Gas stations were springing up in every town, so it was easy enough to sell the gas when we got back near home. Only the barrels we hauled in the back of the Model T truck had false bottoms. They held gas in the top part and looked like they were full, but the bottom could be removed and a keg of whiskey was attached to the bottom. When the barrel was turned upside down, the bottom could be pulled out with the keg of whiskey. The barrels had real bottoms that contained the gas, with a cavity just big enough to conceal the whiskey keg. Each barrel held forty gallons of gas and five gallons of whiskey.

Profit from the gas would pay the expenses of hauling it, but the real profit was the whiskey. We would have to pay five dollars a gallon for it, but we were selling whiskey for two dollars a pint; so there was some money in running whiskey. If caught though, that would be a different story entirely. The trick was not to get caught. I did consider that the profit would outweigh the risk. I packed a bag of clothes, shaving kit, and five hundred dollars in cash to pay for our product. Tubby had been told the boys over Chicago way didn't deal in credit, and I didn't want to drive that far and come back empty handed. It took about all the money we could muster up.

"Sure hope you don't run into some gangster along the way and get robbed," Tubby called out as I was climbing into the Model T. There had been a lot of talk about organized crime in Chicago, so I was a bit apprehensive about going there. I had lived with some rough hombres when I did time in Leavenworth. Most of the boys there had done bad things but weren't so bad. I learned that there is even a little honor among thieves.

I was back on the road again. This time in a truck that went about half as fast as my roadster, but it could haul more than ten times as much whiskey and wasn't near as conspicuous. Women were attracted to the roadster but so were the revenuers. I had outran and outmaneuvered them boys by running on back roads and ditching my hooch before they caught up to me or by driving across terrain that was too rough for them to follow. They were good at being a complete nuisance, but I had managed to avoid getting caught with any evidence. So far I had been lucky. I'm not saying the revenuers didn't stop me, because they did stop me several times; they just couldn't pin me with anything outside of the realm of the law except speeding and that wasn't jail-threatening, just hefty fines.

I was to stop at a speakeasy in a suburb on the west side of Chicago and ask for a fellow by the name of Frank. A speakeasy was just a bar where you had to know someone or say a password to get in the door. You had to talk softly I guess so the neighbors wouldn't hear you. I was just to wait there until he came to me. I memorized his name and the name of the speakeasy so as not to leave any paper trail in case I ran into any Prohibition agents along the way. I knew that giving up his name would put me in a lot hotter water with the boys back east than anything the revenuers could dish out. It took three days to make it to my destination with the Model T truck. It was getting late in the day, more like early into the night, when I stepped through a dim outer room into another room with a long bar and no shortage of booze on display. I asked if "Frank" was about. The bartender didn't say anything but walked to a table at the back side of the bar and spoke to a fellow sitting there.

Right away that fellow came along side of me at the bar and said, "I'm Frank. Are you that cowpoke from South Dakota who was sent here to pick up a few barrels of gas?"

I nodded my head and as we shook hands, said, "Bob Gilland is my name." Frank was trailed by a couple of fellows, but they didn't speak and he didn't introduce them.

Frank looked at his boys, saying, "My boys will take your truck and get it loaded for you. Come with me. You can stay at my shack for the night." Frank's boys without a word went out the door. By the time Frank and I made it outside, his fellows had fired up my truck and drove off.

"Didn't get my change of clothes out before they took off," I said to Frank feeling somewhat concerned.

Frank grinned and said, "Don't worry about your clothes; they will still be right where you left them."

"I hope so because the money to pay you for the gas was inside my clothes. I'd heard people get robbed in Chicago," I said more or less asking a question.

"Your belongings will be okay in the truck with my boys," he said reassuringly. "One of the girls will round up some fresh clothes for you when we got over to my place." Seeing Frank's car made me wonder a bit. If his car was that fancy, what would his shack be like? Frank knew his way around, but Chicago, it seemed, was a tad bigger than Thunder Hawk. We went speeding down one street, then another for the better part of an hour when we pulled into an alley and parked in a little parking place.

"Come on; this is my place. I like to use the back door—easier to find parking than out front," he explained. We were walking toward a tall building; it was on the dark side, but there were streetlights far off and a red light above the door to Frank's shack. I had noticed a shadow of a man lurking along the building we were walking toward when we had pulled in to park but didn't say anything. Sudden-like, I seen this fellow come running behind with a knife in his hand pointed right at Frank's back. I did a fast turnaround, grabbing that fellow's wrist with the knife in it with one hand and striking his knife arm at the elbow bending it up against his chest. As I was trying to get the knife, Frank came around, grabbing that fellow's knife arm giving it a jerk. The knife blade went slashing right across the attacking fellow's throat; then blood started spurting. I stepped back, letting go of the fellow. He just went down on his knees, dropping the knife and grabbing his throat with both hands, but blood came oozing out anyway. In a short while, the fellow with the cut throat just toppled over on the street, looking dead.

Frank pulled me by the arm, saying, "Thanks. Let's get inside and get you cleaned up. My boys will deal with that backstabber later. That could've been me lying there instead of him. Good thing for me that you saw him coming up behind us. He's a goon I recognized from a long time ago—he slashed my brother Al across the face back when we were kids in Brooklyn. Didn't expect to see him here, though."

We went inside, and it was a far cry from any shack that I had ever seen. It was fancier than any nightclub I'd seen in Paris or other parts during the war. There was an orchestra playing music, a dining area, and bar with gals waiting tables in very skimpy clothing. Some shack. We found an empty table and before we even sat down, a gal was there wanting to know what she could get us. Frank looking at me said, "Why don't you go to the washroom and clean up a little? Looks like you just came from butcherin' chickens." I did as he said. I had blood spattered all over the front side of me. Frank didn't have a spot of blood on him that I could see; guess he had been more street savvy than me. We were polishing off a large steak when we had a visitor stroll over to our table. I thought it must be his brother Al when I saw the big scar across one side of his face. Frank, pointing at me, said, "Al, you are looking at the man who got your revenge for that scar you are carrying. That punk from Brooklyn is lying out back with his throat cut, thanks to Bob here." Al shook my hand heartily saying that he was much obliged. "We left Brooklyn to get away from that kind. He got what he deserved in coming here. Thank you my friend."

I stammered, "It was more Frank's doing. I was just stopping that fellow from sticking a knife in Frank's back."

"Cowboy, you did us a favor and we won't forget. Make yourself to home here," Al replied. Then he motioned one good-looking, little red-haired gal to come over, saying to her, "Take Bob upstairs and make him comfortable. He's our guest." Then he said to me, "See you tomorrow, have a good night." I couldn't help but feeling there was something familiar about Al, like I'd seen him before. But that couldn't be as I'd never been to Chicago before and he sure had never been to the reservation. Frank left with Al, so with my escort (Roxie was her name) at my side, we headed for a bath and a bed upstairs. It was midmorning before I woke. I noticed right away that my clothes were gone—my Hyer cowboy boots were by the bed and my black Stetson was sitting on a chair, but no clothes. I was still pondering the situation when Roxie came in with some fancy duds.

"I sent your clothes to the burning barrel; they were stained with ketchup or somethin'. Hope you don't mind. Here're some clothes to get you by, in case you want to get out of bed today." The clothes fit and I felt quite sharp in my new three-piece, striped suit and my black boots and Stetson, but I was wondering if I had enough money with me to pay for them.

Roxie must have read my mind. She said, "Don't worry about paying for the clothes. Frank said not to take any money from you for anything. Let's go eat. I'll show you a good café near here." Roxie was right; the café did have good food.

We were about to leave when in waltzes Frank. Sitting down at our table he said, "You look good in that rig. Now that you're wearin' a suit, we were wonderin' if you'd do us a favor. We need a load of gas delivered over to Detroit. That's if you ain't in a big hurry to get back to the reservation. We'll deduct fifty bucks off the price of your load of gas if you make this run for us. You leave now, you can be back by evening."

It didn't take long for me to figure that would be good money for half a day's driving. "Sure," I said, "but where, exactly, is my truck?

Frank grinned at my comment, then looking at Roxie, said, "Catch a cab and take him over to our refinery—go with him on the run if you want to."

Roxie nodded. "Sure thing Frank." As the taxi came to a stop, Roxie said softly, "This is it." The building had North Side Garage painted across its front. It didn't look like much of a refinery to me, but a truck was sitting there loaded with barrels. Roxie pointed to the truck and said, "That is our load."

"I thought I would be driving my truck, but guess I can drive that one. I drove an ambulance back in the army. My .38 is back in my truck and I would feel a little better having it with me in case someone tries a hijacking."

"They're probably still loading your truck, but I have a little pea shooter in my purse. Here take this. It's loaded, you just have to flip this safety off." She said handing me a little pistol.

I took her weapon, sticking it under my belt. "Guess it beats nothing, just hope we won't need it." Roxie knew the roads to take, so she was welcome company, but she would have been welcome to ride with me even if she didn't know the way. She was a pretty gal and she dressed nice. Looking over at her, I said, "I think you look prettier in those cloths than the skimpy ones you wore last night."

Roxie looked over at me smiling. "I suppose you're wondering what a nice girl like me is doing working in a nightclub. Well, growing up in Chicago hasn't been all roses. My dad's a bum, and my mother had to start selling herself to support me and my two little sisters. We never had much money. I never learned any other skills. I did wait tables at a café and I had different low paying jobs, but I make more money in one night at the club than I made in a month at those other jobs. My little sisters are getting educated by what I do, so they can get honest jobs. I think the end results outweigh the means. Some day when I have lots of money, I'd like to settle in with a nice guy and give up this kind of life. What about you—are you a real cowboy? What do you want out of life?"

I told her a little of my story. "I grew up on an Indian reservation with four brothers and three sisters. My mother is Indian and my dad is a Scotchman. Two brothers and a sister have passed, and life hasn't been real easy for me either. My folks raised kids, cattle, and horses, so about all I know is cowboy stuff. I did go off to that war we just had and when I got out I didn't have many cattle left and not much money, so I got into running moonshine. I've made more money at this than I could make at being a cowboy. One day I'll go back to raising cattle, maybe find a pretty gal to settle in with, too."

Roxie pointed to a stop sign coming up as she said, "Just about there, turn at that stop sign, then it is only a mile to the garage where we drop off the gas." I slowed the truck to a stop but before I turned, the door on Roxie's side of the truck was jerked open. I had caught a glimpse of a figure coming out of the trees by the side of the road, so instinctively I slipped Roxie's little pistol into my left hand and flipped the safety off.

The guy pointed a pistol right at me and ordered, "Get out right now and walk over to them trees or I'll slug you right where you sit." My thought was that is some choice: if I walk to the trees, he will just shoot me in the back so might as well not do that. Without a word, I just pointed the pistol in my hand at his face and squeezed the trigger. He went back toward the ditch in a zip; his reflexes pulled off a round but it went high of me and through the top of the cab of the truck. He hit the ditch looking like his hijacking days were over and his life too. Roxie closed the door, I just eased on around the corner, and we went on about our task of delivering gas. We had only gone a half mile or so before we came upon a road block: two fancy black cars parked crossways on the road ahead.

"Roxie, this must be our lucky day, looks like revenuers," I said bringing the truck to a stop.

Two men came prancing right up to the truck and asked, "What are you hauling cowboy?"

"Gasoline. Just taking it to that gas station up ahead. Is there a problem?" I answered quickly.

"Not if you're right, but we got a tip that this truck was hauling moonshine. If you don't mind, we'll just check the barrels." Before I had time to answer them boys, they were up in the back of the truck opening the bungs on the barrels. After they found gas in all the barrels, they politely stepped off the truck, saying, "Sorry for the delay, but we had to check. You can go."

They moved their cars and I went on to the gas station. Roxie said that there was a loading dock at the back side of the station. "Just back up to it and they will unload it for us."

I did as she said and as I stepped from the truck, a grubby looking cuss came out muttering, "About time," as he handed me an envelope.

I took the envelope and started counting the money. Grubby waved a couple of lads over; they had one barrel off the truck when I said, "Hold your horses there boys. The money count is off. That's only half of what it is supposed to be. Either come up with the rest of the money or load that barrel back on this truck."

"I'll pay the rest after we sell the gas," the grubby fellow replied.

"No, that won't work," I said. "Frank made it very clear that he didn't do business on credit, and I can't afford to pay the difference from my wages." Grubby looked mad, but he seemed to know that I wasn't bluffing. Roxie waved her hand out the window of the truck with her pistol in her hand, which might have been more persuasive than me. He mumbled something, then handed me the rest of the money. Didn't take long to be on the road again heading back to Chicago by a different way that Roxie knew bypassing the road where we had left the aspiring hijacker laying in the ditch.

My partner in crime hadn't said much but now she came out with, "Ever kill anyone before?"

I thought about lying to her and saying no but, I didn't; I answered, "Yes, I have. I did seven years in the pen for shooting my cousin in a drunken fight. I didn't intend to kill him, and I likely didn't, one of the other boys shot him. Then I went over to the war as a soldier for a couple of years. When you are lying in a trench with enemy throwing bullets in the vicinity of where you are, I have to say you want to shoot back. How many men I shot in the war I can't say, but sure I did in a few." Roxie seemed satisfied with that answer, and we just talked about the weather the rest of the way back to Chicago. It was some after dark when we drove up to the North Side Garage. We got a taxi and Roxie had the cabby drop us off behind the nightclub; like Frank, she preferred using the back door to the place. This time there wasn't any goon lurking around and the one that had been there the night before was gone. Maybe the boys took him to places unknown.

Frank was sitting at a table when we walked in, so we joined him. I handed him his money. He didn't count it, just stuck it in a pocket. "Thanks. Your load will be ready in the morning. Roxie make our cowboy comfortable tonight. He has a long way to drive back to South Dakota tomorrow." We ordered some food and Frank headed for the door, but Roxie caught up to him at the door and they talked for a few minutes.

Frank left and Roxie came back to the table. "The run today was just a test to see if they could trust you. I told Frank you passed the test. He said he would have his boys clean up that mess in the road ditch and have a few words with that dink at that gas station."

"Some test," I said a little angrily. "It could have gotten us killed!"

Roxie just smiled at that and said, "You know what they say about war—no risk, no glory!"

Morning came early with Roxie literally rolling me out of bed. It was time to head on back home to Thunder Hawk. My truck was loaded and sitting out front of the North Side Garage when we got there. I checked my truck for my money and pistol; everything was just as Frank said it would be. Roxie gave me a big parting kiss, and I handed her the money for the load, but she didn't take it. She said Frank told her to tell me that it was "on the house." I cranked up the truck and headed back to my reservation, thinking Frank and Al may be gangsters of some sort, but they sure are swell enough fellows in my book—probably just don't want to get on their bad side.

I made it back to Thunder Hawk without crossing trails with any more revenuers, and Tubby was sure glad to see me come rolling into his yard with the barrels of "gas." Tubby had the details worked out to sell the gas at the station in Thunder Hawk for a good profit, and he had Ray Bammble at the local hardware store order several cases of pint bottles, which he had taken to the farm earlier. We could make beer for our own use, just couldn't sell it, so we had to have a good many bottles to put it in—that was

Tubby's story anyway. We siphoned off the gas at the station, and then took the truck out to Tubby's farm. Then we upended the gas barrels and removed the whiskey carrying it down into the secret room in the well. After we had all the whiskey stashed, we filled a case of bottles with whiskey and sent Todd Kruze on a run to Rapid City.

CHAPTER 13

The Rapid City Run

Todd always had a good-looking woman with him in the car. Either his wife or another woman. I didn't ask. I got to thinking about his taking a woman passenger along and came to the conclusion that he had a good idea. Effie Quay lived just east of Thunder Hawk, and we had been friends a long while. She was one of the group of us breed Indian kids from around Thunder Hawk who had gone to Indian school together. Effie was nice, not as pretty as some but not bad to look at either. She knew that I traveled around to different places from my taking her to a few social functions in my roadster and telling some of my experiences. She had told me that she would like to go with me sometime when I went to the Black Hills as she had never been there before. I loaded up my roadster with a case of whiskey and stopped at the Quay place. Effie was still living at home with her parents but worked at the school in Keldron a few miles to the east. Keldron was another new town that came to be with homesteading. She could speak Lakota and English, so the school hired her to teach the Indian kids and breeds how to speak English.

When I told Effie that I was heading for Deadwood and asked her if she wanted to ride along, saying we could do some sightseeing, she exclaimed, "I can be ready to go in five minutes. I just need to be back for school by Monday."

Since it was Friday, I said that was fine and we could be back Sunday afternoon. We traveled right along getting to Newell in time to grab a bite to eat and a fill-up of gas. As I was waiting to pay for the gas, a gent in front of me mumbled to the man at the counter, "Damned federal agents had the road blocked coming down Boulder Canyon, checking every vehicle. Took me an extra hour just to get over here."

I hadn't told my passenger that I had a load of whiskey in the trunk of the roadster. As we were leaving Newell, I confessed, "I'm going to go the long way to Deadwood over to Belle Fourche and come into Deadwood from the west side. There's a case of whiskey in the trunk. If we're stopped by the law, we would likely be arrested, so it would be best not to get caught."

Effie didn't seem surprised. She just said, "I figured as much; I knew there had to be a reason for all your traveling." We did make it to Deadwood without getting stopped, but it was ways into the night by the time we got unloaded. My gal, Effie, did get to see a lot more of the Black Hills than I had planned, and she was awed at how roads were built through the mountains and how people could have houses right on hillsides. We got a room at the Franklin Hotel and didn't go out on the town. That Effie really had a way of warming up a bed. She went to sleeping and didn't even snore that I heard. I dozed off to sleep thinking, "She can eat crackers in my bed anytime and I wouldn't complain." I woke suddenly, with Effie screaming and thrashing around in the bed. It was scary and I wasn't sure what to do but I grabbed her and held her. In a little, her screams turned to whimpers and she woke, asking, "Did I hurt you?"

I whispered, "No, but you sure seemed to be having a battle with someone."

"I'm sorry, but I have these dreams over and over about when I was thirteen back at that Indian school," Effie whimpered at first, but her voice grew stronger as she told me about the dark terror of her boarding school days. "A Father McClure at the school, at least once a week, would call in one of us girls to his room and make us undress and explain our female parts in English. He said he was making us learn to speak English and teaching us the facts of life, and then he would proceed with laying us down on his bed and having intercourse with us. He had done that with many of the girls there. We all feared our day with him, but there was not a thing any of us could do about it. No one would listen or do anything about it, and when we tried to tell, we were severely punished by the Sisters who were in charge of our dorm.

"One of the girls told our friend Brave Bear about what was happening, and the night Father McClure was having his way with me, Brave Bear, with the help of some of the other girls distracting the Sister Nuns, slipped into Father McClure's room. Father McClure was so occupied by what he was doing to me that he didn't hear Brave Bear come in. Brave Bear tomahawked Father McClure ending his rape. He just went limp and was completely dead and still lying on top of me. I first got my clothes back on, then with the help of Brave Bear, and two other girls, we wrapped our good father in a blanket, boosted him out the window from his room, and carried him down to the river. It was in the dead of winter and the ice was thick, but Brave Bear knew where there was an air hole, where there wasn't any ice, so we just threw Father McClure into that air hole and he disappeared into the night.

"Brave Bear stayed calm through it all. Although he was just a boy, he spoke in a firm voice, saying, 'Give me time to get gone. Then go back to your dorm and tell that you jumped out of Father McClure's window when he tried to molest you, and he chased you down to the river. Say you ran around the thin ice, but he didn't. He just ran right into that air hole and disappeared.' I did as Brave Bear had said, and Father Reed, the head of the school, said he thought I might be right, but keep it quiet until Father McClure comes back to dispute my story. Father McClure never did come back and no one missed him, especially not us girls. Father Reed just passed his death off as an accident on the ice. All the girls at the school owed Brave Bear a great favor and none told about what happened. I'm sorry, but I still have bad dreams about that night with Father McClure."

I said softly, "Sounds like you did the right thing, so don't dwell on it. Life isn't always a bed of roses. We meet bad people with manipulative minds who use others for their own evil ends—people who cheat, lie, steal, and we just deal with them the best we can and get on with our lives. Sitting Bull said, 'We can no longer live in our world but have to live in both worlds (the white world and the Indian world). If something is good for our people, then pick it up but, if it is not good for our people, then to just let it be.' I'm guessing that would hold true for people as well. By that theory I suppose we shouldn't be running moonshine either. We aren't making our people pick it up, but they do. So the way I see it, I might as well make some money from the moonshine runs as someone else."

Effie whispered, "You're right. Thank you. Let's get some sleep." This time I went to sleep thinking maybe I talk too much!

I did get Effie home by Sunday night a little after dark. We came back by way of Hill City, then Rapid City, staying at Interior, a town east of Rapid City on the Pine Ridge Reservation. Effie seen some of the Black Hills along with the Badlands of South Dakota. We were stopped in Scenic, a little town southeast of Rapid City, by some G-boys, but they didn't find any hooch in the roadster; so they politely let us travel on. Them revenuer boys were sure making their presence in Indian country well known, but they weren't well liked, so the word got around fast if they were spotted in an area, and most times a runner with moonshine had time to bypass their stakeouts.

CHAPTER 14

The Preacher's Friend

In spite of the hound-dogging revenuers and other Prohibition agents, we made a lot of runs and were soon out of hooch again. This time I made a run to Canada, and to avoid North Dakota, I went through the west side of Minnesota using a lot of back trails. I was coming down the road just cruising along in real flat country a little outside of Aberdeen, South Dakota, when about a half mile down the road, I could see cars lined up and stopping, so I turned into a farm road and went into the farmer's yard. Thought I would just wait until they left, or go back and find another road. Well, the farmer came out and we got to talking. He told me his name was David Iverson, and he came up with a plan because he didn't like those revenuers either. He knew a back road that he used to go to the Lutheran Church each Sunday with his team and buggy. His wife and daughter had went over to the church earlier to help clean it for Sunday service. He would ride over there with me and if we got stopped, he would introduce me as their new minister. He figured if we started talking about coming to church to the revenuers, they might not do much searching. The church was over at the edge of the town of Bowdle, west of Aberdeen and past the roadblock. If we got to the church, then I could go on down the road and he would ride home with his wife. Good plan, I thought.

We were rolling down that back road getting close to the church and I was about to relax thinking his plan worked, when I seen it—a car behind me coming fast with a light a flashing on its top. Well, I was caught, so I just stopped, and that car came right up behind and a big fellow came out of each side of that car. They lost no time at getting alongside of my roadster, one on each side.

Iverson was all smiles and asked, "What we can we do for you gentlemen?"

The gent on the farmer's side said, "We're searching for illegal whiskey. There seems to be a lot of it being smuggled into South Dakota. Maybe you just took this back road to avoid our roadblock."

"Oh well, sorry to disappoint you boys then," Iverson said, "but this here is our new preacher, come from Iowa. I'm a deacon at our church and he and his wife came to visit. The girls went over to clean our church earlier and we were just going over to join them." Then he brought up his Bible that he had lying between us on the seat, and said, looking over at me, "Brother Bob here will be giving a real interesting sermon tomorrow morning starting at ten o'clock at that church right up ahead, about hell and damnation, and we would really like to see you boys joining us." Then without hesitation he asked, "Do you boys believe in God?"

The one on my side nodded yes, and the one on the farmer's side was looking very uncomfortable and was squirming around but he finally said in a real soft voice, "Yes, yes I do."

Iverson really looked delighted now and said, "That is the first step, now then listen to this." He had his Bible marked to a chapter that was about going to church, and he started to reading, "All sinners must repent and come to the house of the Lord and gain strength from the Lord by getting down on their knees and praying." And he didn't stop there, he said, "If you boys can't make it to our service, we'd be glad to get out and kneel down and pray with you now," and he started to open his door. Well that cinched it. The fellow on my side suddenly remembered that they had a meeting back at Aberdeen and they were late, so they really had to be going. They abruptly hustled back to their car and spun it around and were going the other way about as fast as they had come.

I sure thanked Iverson, as I dropped him off at his church. However, as I was just leaving, the prettiest young gal came out of that church and waved. I waved back but kept going. I did think though that if that was my implied wife, maybe I should just take up preaching. It was easy, didn't even have to do any talking. Nevertheless, I just shifted the gears and was back on the road again. After that run, I just quit going to Canada because it was a lot easier to run the gas truck to Chicago and less likely to get caught. The car was faster, but with it, I had to take all the back roads driving a lot of extra miles. One run with the truck brought back ten times as much hooch as the car.

I told Tubby that I thought we should make just short runs with the roadster and he agreed. "I have enough money in the bank now to buy some land and enough cattle to make an honest living," I said, and after some thinking, I added, "this run is going to be my last." I had been out of the army for five years now and that life was fading from my memories. But, like Effie, I still woke some nights in a dead sweat haunted by memories of death and war.

Getting caught at this job started looking more likely, too. The last run I did to Deadwood was a little on the side of a close call. I made it a practice to check the delivery place over before I delivered. It was early evening when I drove into Deadwood. I parked the Roaster a block from the Wild Bill Saloon, where I was to deliver a case of whiskey. As I walked toward the Wild Bill, I spotted a shiny new Buick with two fellows sitting in it. When I walked inside, two fellows sharply dressed in city clothes were sitting at a back table reading newspapers. My thoughts were that they were federal agents sure as the devil—no one else would go to a bar to read a newspaper. So I just ordered a Sarsaparilla; the bar was mostly empty, but one of the gals working there came over sitting down by me. We made the usual small talk, and then I asked her if she wanted to get out of here and go with me over to Rapid City to a dance. She was quick to say, "Sure," and then added, "but I need to run to my room first and put on some nicer clothes."

"It's no bother. I don't mind waiting for you," I answered. After sipping on my pop for twenty minutes and finishing it, then waiting another ten minutes or so, back comes my barmaid date looking completely different. She was wearing a kind of soft, purple-colored dress that showed off her long legs and her figure to some advantage. She had a matching hat and a slinky fur at her neck that looked an awful lot like the minks that Brave Bear and I used to trap along the Grand River in the winter. Most of the girls I'd known working in bars couldn't afford expensive duds like those. As we were walking toward the door to leave, she looked over at the revenuer with a big smile that confirmed my suspicion she was working with them or, in fact, she was one of them herself. Well, I thought if she insists on looking in my car the jig's up for me, but I might as well enjoy my freedom until she does. I had parked my car up the street near the Franklin Hotel and as we were nearing my car, we could hear music coming from across the street at the Old Style Number 10 Saloon, so I said to my fancy-dressed gal, "Sounds like a dance in progress at the Old Style. Let's just go there, save driving clear to Rapid City." We walked into a crowd of people at the Old Style and went to dancing. The gal with the fancy clothes called herself Jane Smith; she said she was from back east and had come to Deadwood with a friend to try mining gold. The mine had no jobs for women, but her fellow hired on, and she had taken a job at the Wild Bill. Her friend didn't like the mine work, and when they had a disagreement, he just left town without her.

As we were walking from the dance floor looking for an empty table, I had a tap on the shoulder. I turned to see who was tapping on my shoulder, hoping it wasn't either a jealous boyfriend, some drunk miner just wanting to be tough, or a revenuer. Turns out it was Danny Williams, one of the fellows from Lemmon I knew pretty well. He had bootlegged whiskey for us at different times. After I introduced him to Jane, he said that he wanted to borrow my car to run a friend of his home. He went on to tell that his friend, Joe Pakaama, had rode his horse to work at the mine and tied it to a tree, but when he was done working, his horse had gotten loose. He lived south of Deadwood about ten miles and figured his horse just went back home, so he needed a ride.

I usually didn't let others drive my roadster, but Danny seemed desperate and he was a good friend, so I just handed him my keys, saying, "Okay, but no reckless driving. I figure to get a room at the

Franklin Hotel, so just park it close to here, and bring the keys to my room."

"Thanks. I already got a room at the Franklin. You can share it if you want." He handed me the key to his room, adding, "I'll get a key from the night clerk if I get there first." With that sorted out, Danny left and Jane and I found a table but were soon back dancing. She liked to dance and was good at what she liked. The dance came to an end and Danny still hadn't returned. I didn't see my car parked anywhere.

As I was walking Jane back to her room over at the Wild Bill, she quietly said, "A night cap would sure go good tonight. Would you like to come up to my room for a night cap?"

I thought, "That is a dumb question, lady," but I answered, "Sure, but I don't think there's any whiskey to be found in this whole town."

She smiled and answered, "You might be surprised." She led me up a stairway going up the side of the Wild Bill to her room. We went in and there sitting on a stand was a flask of whiskey. Jane poured us a night cap, and then said in a soft voice, "You can sleep here if you want. They say it isn't safe to walk the streets alone in this town late at night."

I thought, "You don't have to ask me twice," but I didn't say anything, just sat down pulling off my boots.

Jane then added, "In case you're wondering, I just work in the bar. My boyfriend left over a month ago, and you're the first I've invited to my room since he left."

I awoke in Jane's bed alone. I figured she must have went to breakfast or work. Morning already being quite a tad bit past first light, I jumped back into my duds and did a fast walk to the Franklin Hotel. Danny came strolling in just as I was handing the clerk the key to his room. He said that he slept at a friend's house. "It was late when I got back to town, and her place was closer than this hotel. I had a flat on your car last night, too. I just threw the tire in the trunk, but I'll get it fixed for you after we go eat breakfast." The nearest café was just up the street and as we were walking to it, I asked Danny how he happened to get himself stranded in Deadwood. With a big grin on his face, he answered, "I have my car, but I seen those guys at the Will Bill and sittin' in parked cars. And that Two-Gun Hart had been nosing around. I knew they must had been tipped off. I thought up a way to stash the hooch while they were watching you. By the way, that gal you were with last night works for them. She's busted quite a few moonshiners already. She's good at what she does. Hope you didn't tell her anything that might get us in trouble."

"I figured as much. She asked a lot of questions. I didn't tell her anything about our business that could be used by her. Just talked about cattle ranching till she couldn't take anymore. I agree she's good at what she does." Danny went with me in the roadster to get the tire fixed. We stopped at a little gas station that happened to be open on Sunday morning where they could fix the tire. Just as I opened the trunk, four federal agents were right there, peeking over my shoulder. Looking at the nearest one, I said, "Sorry boys but I need get this flat tire out of this trunk." Hoisting the tire from the trunk, I said to the fellow looking at me, "Now go ahead and look until your heart's content." Those revenuers were very thorough but didn't find a thing. Disappointed, they all left.

When they were gone, Danny then said, "The hooch is safe with Joe Pakaama. I've bootlegged booze to Joe at different times. He's as honest as the day is long though he's poor as all get out. He doesn't have the money to pay for the whiskey that just happened to get stashed at his place, but within a week he'll get the whiskey sold and have the money for us."

Danny went to explain how it all worked. "Joe has a good source of demand for the whiskey in the miners. All the miners carry lunch boxes to work. Joe packs his with pints of whiskey, and when he goes home, he just takes the lunch box with payment for the whiskey in it from the miner who wants the whiskey."

"How do they pass all those lunch boxes around without being noticed? I asked.

"Joe has an old Model T and he gives a lift to work to several miners. That makes trading lunch pails around simple and easy with nobody any the wiser."

I had packed twenty-five fifths and forty pints of whiskey in the roadster, but that was only a tenth of what we carried back on our gas runs. Nevertheless, it was still a lot of money to trust in the hands of someone I didn't know. I just told Danny, "You saved my bacon on this one and if you trust Joe, then fine with me." I dropped Danny off at his car and before I drove off, said, "Thanks Danny, see you back home. Keep the money you get from Joe for that load of whiskey." I figured he had earned every penny of that money and I sure would rather he have it than have it confiscated by the revenuer. Danny saving me from doing time in barbwire city, to my kind of thinking, was money well spent.

CHAPTER 15

Know When to Hold 'Em

Tubby had taken up fixing cars for people at his shop building on their farm, a mile northwest of Thunder Hawk. It was mostly a decoy but some legit too. There was always someone stopping at Tubby's garage to get their cars worked on. More often than not it was a bootlegger, and a couple of women were taking to bootlegging too. Maude Williamson ran with her brother Earl some and could peddle whiskey better than her brother could. Arora Duncan drove her own car and could ride a horse and shoot as good as any man. She was on the pretty side too.

When I made it back to Thunder Hawk, I drove over to Tubby's telling him about my trip to Deadwood and that we had a snitch in our midst. We ran through names of our brothers in crime—the other bootleggers in the area—trying to figure out which one might have been the stool pigeon. There were two fellows from McIntosh, Stanton Rye and Cliff Bloski that I didn't know well, but Tubby defended them saying that those boys were no snitches. I mentioned John Harwood and Ed Nehl, and Tubby again said he was sure they weren't the culprits. We went on naming our people but came to the conclusion that they were all trustworthy. Tubby said he thought we had best hold off on any more runs and I agreed with him. However, we had to figure out who squealed to the revenuers, because they sure as heck had been waiting for me in Deadwood. Tubby started talking about a plan to get everyone together in the town hall for some kind of meeting of our "friends," when a rider came galloping into the farmyard. It was Jim on a green horse that he had a little trouble getting a handle on, so, he got off and led the horse over to where we were. I spoke first saying, "If you would work that horse in the round corral first, you would probably get along with it better."

"I didn't ride out here to get advice on how to break a horse," he said somewhat impatiently. "I came to tell you that you need to have a talk with our brother Abe. He and I were at the pool hall in Thunder Hawk a week or so back, and we both got a little liberal with the drinking. And you know Abe, when he drinks, everybody has to drink, as if he was the last of the big spenders. He's been telling about how he masterminded bootlegging all across South Dakota, so he has plenty of money to buy drinks. Hell, he could even by the pool hall if he wanted to." Ploog's Pool Hall was Thunder Hawk's speakeasy where you could buy a drink by the glass or bottle.

Tubby had decided not to give Abe any more whiskey to bootleg because he never brought any money back, but he did know a little about our operation. I hadn't thought he would be dumb enough to talk about it though. "I don't think Abe would deliberately turn us in but if the wrong person heard him talking, we could hang just the same," Tubby mused aloud. Bootlegging wasn't a hanging offense, but the thought of going back to Leavenworth was not one I wanted to entertain.

Jim said that a fellow called John Nelson was rubbing elbows with Abe that night and seemed to be asking Abe a lot of questions. I told Jim that I most nigh met my Waterloo with my Deadwood whiskey run. I relayed the whole story, including how Danny Williams helped me out of a tight spot.

"I'm sure John Nelson is your snitch. I knew there was a reason I didn't cotton up to him much," Jim sputtered out with a rough edge in his voice. "Nelson had been talking just a little too cozy with that fancy-dressed Prohibition agent Two-Gun Hart."

"I'd thought there was something phony about Hart all along, but I couldn't quite put my finger on it. He tried to pass himself off as some kind of Oglala Indian, but he was always complaining about how "breeds" shouldn't be dealing booze. Not drinking it, but dealing it," I added.

Tubby said sharply, "In that case, we need to deal with Nelson before we move any more hooch." Tubby reached behind some tools for the pint he kept stashed in the shop and passed it around. We all had a couple of hearty sips, then he placed it back in hiding, wiping it clean before he did. He said nowadays the revenuers have figured out how to take fingerprints off things and can catch lawbreakers just by their fingerprints. I hadn't known that but I thought that's good to know. "Bob you can make a dry run back to Deadwood and tip off that revenue gal you know. Jim you can ride around and get the word to our people: there will be no bootlegging booze from us at the dance at the Town Hall here in Thunder Hawk this Saturday night. I'll have a couple of the boys slip a part of a case of moonshine in the manger of Nelson's barn, and that pint we just drank part of, with another pint, under the seat of his truck. That should put our informer in good with the revenuers!"

The Deadwood trail was getting to be a boring one, especially with doing a dry run, so I asked Arora Duncan to ride along to keep me company. She was willing to go, saying she had nothing better to do, seeing as how Tubby had put a hold on our business venture. I had been seeing Arora some so had told her about the details with that John Nelson along with the reason I needed to make the run to Deadwood. We headed for Deadwood, leaving Thunder Hawk but didn't get far. About three miles west of Thunder Hawk, just past Vern Labioa's place sat a couple of big black touring-style cars with revenuers poised to stop and search any passing car or truck. I knew the routine well; I pulled over, and within a jiffy, we were out of the roadster with them boys looking for moonshine.

I thought, "This might be a good time to talk about Nelson," but Arora spoke up before I could, "I think I know what you fellows are looking for. Abe Gilland's wife Viola is a friend of mine. When he came home drunk the other night she was madder than a wet hen at Abe for being drunk again. She said that Abe told her he had gotten the whiskey from John Nelson and that John had enough whiskey stashed in his barn to get the whole town of Thunder Hawk drunk." Then she flashed her best smile at them.

I tried to look irritated and whispered kinda loud to Arora, "That's probably just drunk talk. I don't know John Nelson well, but he appears to be an upright citizen who will surely take offense to a story like that!"

Arora came back like she was arguing with me, "You're probably right, but Abe got whiskey from someone because Viola said he sure was drunk, and she wouldn't lie to me."

Right away, one of the agents asked Arora, "Where can we find this John Nelson?"

"I don't know where he lives, but he always comes to dances in this area, and there is one in Thunder Hawk Saturday night," offered Arora along with that smile. They seemed to have bought Arora's story, and they waved us on down the road. We drove on to Lemmon, but I told Arora that I didn't think we needed to drive to Deadwood. We went shopping at Freymark's Clothing Store in Lemmon instead. On the way back to Arora's place, I asked her if she'd like to go with me to the Saturday night dance in Thunder Hawk.

"Sure," she said without hesitation, "I wouldn't miss that dance for the world."

A good-size crowd of folks had already gathered at the Town Hall in Thunder Hawk, and Dad and his band boys were playing music. As Arora and I were walking toward the hall, Abe came walking out with his arm around John Nelson's shoulder and acting as if he already had one too many. Abe spoke loud enough for us to hear, saying, "Come on Johnny boy. Let's go out to that fancy new pickup truck of yours and have us a snort." No sooner than they'd climbed into John's Model T pickup from nowhere came a flock of federal agents. In nothing flat they had Abe and John out of the truck and pulled out two pints of whiskey from under the seat.

John looked a bit taken aback and totally surprised, saying, "I don't know where that came from. Abe must have put it there!"

One of the revenuers calmly said, "That's what they all say. Come along with us." They then proceed to go over the Nelson's barn and quickly uncovered the half case in the manger. "There's just a little too much booze here for a Saturday night nip," deadpanned the agent. "It's clear you have been transporting and selling it."

Abe got off with a hefty fine, but Nelson found himself doing some time in the jailhouse.

CHAPTER 16

Cowpoking to Sioux City

We still all had a few cattle, and it was time to ship some of the cattle to the market, but we were all short on money. A new shipping yard came to be at Sioux City, Iowa, shortening the trip, so the cattle were to be railed to Sioux City rather than Chicago. Dad made a deal with several other ranchers to bring in their cattle too, so we would have enough to fill two boxcars with cattle. Each car could haul forty head of mature cattle or fifty-five head of yearlings, give or take. He had told them that Jim and I would ride in the boxcars as cowpokes. When cattle were shipped by rail, they had a habit of lying down in the boxcar. If they did, other cattle would trample them, so someone had to ride in the car with them. The cowpoke stood on a platform in one corner of the boxcar with a long pole to poke any cattle that laid down, making them get up again. We would also read brands when we got there, so each person would get the right cattle sold in their names.

Dad might be getting old, but he still hadn't lost his touch at finding something for his boys to do, and maybe he thought I was spending a little too much time driving around in Tubby's gas truck. Jim and I were back in the saddle again, helping to bring in cattle for the shipping. Our furthest roundup was at Jake Flying Horse's place southeast of Thunder Hawk near about forty miles.

He only had a dozen two-year old steers to ship but needed help in sorting them off from his herd and trailing them to Thunder Hawk. Jake's son and daughter, Roy and Else, helped out, and they were good help. By the time we had his steers sorted, we were about out of daylight, so we corralled his steers for the night. Jake was a friendly sort and insisted that we stay the night; his wife happened to be a good cook and with darkness coming on, it was easy for Jake to talk Jim and me into spending the night. After a hearty meal, Jim and Else went for a walk down to the river. The Flying Horse place was sitting in a good location for wintering cattle on the north side of the Grand River with trees all around and hills to the north and west of the place.

It was only about fifteen miles further to Chance Duncan's place, south of Morristown, and we had made plans with him to stop with Jim's steers at his place. Chance Duncan had some cattle to ship as well, and he had a small holding pasture to bed the steers down for the night. Jim's steers stayed together, moved out at a fast pace for a mile or so, and then slowed to a good walk. It was a cool fall day, good for trailing cattle, and we made good time and were a couple of miles east of Skull Butte by midday. Chance's place was just a couple of miles to the northwest of Skull Butte.

Two riders came in sight chasing a half-dozen steers in our direction and soon had their steers mingling with the ones we were trailing. It was Arora and a farmer by the name of Henry McKay, who had a homestead a couple of miles to the south, and he wanted to ship his steers too. We let the steers rest a bit while we chatted with McKay and Arora.

"Looks like we have company on our trail," observed Jim.

There were two more riders coming up behind us from the east with a dozen or so steers. The riders were John O'Donnell and Duke McSweeney. When they got close, John rode ahead up to where we were sitting in our saddles. "I was helping McSweeney get his steers over to Chance Duncan's. Do you suppose that we could throw these steers in with yours?" he asked.

"Sure," I answered, "the more the better."

"It's only another five miles to Chance's place. Doesn't look like you will need me. I have plenty of work to do on my homestead," and with that McKay just headed his horse for home. I thought, "Well we really didn't need him anyway."

When we arrived at Chance's, Arora knew right where to leave the steers for the night, in a small pasture to the north of the place. There were quite a few other steers already in that pasture. Chance owned the lion's share but had volunteered to trail half a dozen homesteaders' steers as well. Chance was expecting us and greeted us heartily. "You made good time getting those steers here, but you must be hungry enough eat a bite. Tie your horses in the barn, then come to the house. I'll go see if Evelyn will scare up some grub."

It didn't take us long to get our horses tied in the barn. I for one was hungry enough to eat more than a bite. "I feel like my back bone is rubbing against the inside of my belly button," I said hoping for a good hot dinner."

"Don't worry cowboy," said Chance's wife Evelyn, "we've got enough food here to feed a threshing crew."

After a hearty meal, Jim thanked Evelyn, "That was a great meal Evelyn. Thanks much, now I think I can make it clear to Lyman's place in time for supper."

I had told Herb I would help him trail his steers to Thunder Hawk the next day, and there was still enough daylight left to make it there. We had ponied a couple of fresh horses to Chance's place, leaving them there on our way to Jim Flying Horse's place so he had a fresh horse. It was only fifteen miles or so over to Lyman's so he could ride that distance in an easy couple of hours. McSweeney went home to his homestead six miles to the east of Duncan's over on Dirt Lodge Creek. John O'Donnell said he needed to head home to his place at Keldron, too. He and his brothers had some steers to gather and would have them rounded in by the time we got there with our little bunch of steers. We could go on to Thunder Hawk from there. That left me and Arora to trail the herd to Keldron. Chance volunteered to help chase the herd to John's place. Then John and his brothers would help trail the cattle on to the stockyard at Thunder Hawk.

Arora was the Annie Oakley of Thunder Hawk. She liked to think she could ride, drive, or shoot as good as any man. She was pretty much right about that, but I was more interested in other qualities she had, like how well she prettied herself up, how well she could dance, and she was just easy to be around and work with. I held the notion in the back of my mind somewhere that she would be a good candidate for a wife when I had enough money saved up and enough cattle to make an honest living, but I didn't tell her that. Arora and I could have trailed the steers, but we didn't turn down Chance's offer—he too was a good hand on a horse, not like some of those farm boys that impersonated cowboys. To each his own, I didn't do well at impersonating farm boys either.

The girls went to cleaning the kitchen and clearing off the table while Chance and I sat talking about the good old days. "Sure liked it better when we were boys and didn't have to contend with all these homesteaders. Some are all right Joes, but some are sure riffraff characters. There has been more rustling and stealing as of late, and the law seems to be more bent on catching moonshiners and bootleggers than thieves," said Chance offering his strong views.

"Yes," I agreed, "I know firsthand how the law is always chasing moonshiners. I think they must get a kickback from the revenuers, so I suppose there's more money in catching illegal whiskey runners than chicken thieves."

"The grapevine has it that some agents thought they had you caught down Deadwood way a while back. Maybe you should find a different line of work. Once you get them boys on your trail, they watch you like a buzzard waiting for a sick animal to die," said Chance.

"Them boys aren't all boys—one was a woman and she had latched onto me like a tick. I think that's good advice," I told him. "Only problem with that is since the homesteaders came along, there isn't much in the way of honest work in these parts. I don't know how to farm, though reckon I could learn. I think working for a farmer would be harder than busting rock in the pen, and I didn't think much of that."

I rambled on, "Breaking horses is a lost cause too. The horse market has dwindled to a little over nothing with cars and tractors coming in. I figure to try making a living with cattle, but it takes money to get a herd put together. Free grazing went out with the homesteaders coming in. I didn't make any money in the pen or army either for that matter. The bank closing down took care of all I'd saved up from my moonshine runs. That's just money lost."

As Chance and I went on talking, I came to a decision. "I do believe, and it is a unanimous decision on my part, I will not make any more runs to Deadwood."

Chance allowed as how that was probably a good idea and then told me he was trying out another kind of ranching. "I'm giving sheep a go. You get two paying crops a year from sheep—wool and lambs. You can run four sheep on the same amount of grass as a cow, and sheep are easier to handle."

"If sheep didn't blat all the time, I might give them consideration, but that dang blatting in nothing flat would really get on my nerves," I said.

"Be that it may," Chance said, "they do make me more money than the cattle. I just hired a deaf guy—you might know him, Deafy Thompson—to herd the sheep, and they get along fine. Another thing, there aren't any wolves left in this area and very few coyotes. The homesteaders were having a lot of problems with wolves at first, but they came up with the plan of encircling the area where there was a wolf kill with men with shotguns. The men walked in on the wolves, shooting every wolf, coyote, or stray dog, even fox. Now there just aren't any more wolves and very few coyotes, so it's a lot safer to run sheep."

"That's good, wolves didn't just kill sheep. When I was a lad herding Dad's cattle, I heard a cow bawling in a little draw; when I rode over to the spot, a pack of wolves had hamstrung a cow and were feasting on her behind. The cow was still alive with her whole back end ate out. I emptied my pistol on the wolves and then reloaded and shot the cow," I said remembering a little too much what wolves were like.

Evelyn and Arora had finished cleaning the kitchen, and Evelyn asked in her soft voice, "Do you boys want to play a little cards?" Arora poured us each a glass of her favorite moonshine and a hot game of whist was soon under way. The girls beat Chance and me three straight games. I don't think Chance gave it his best, but if we had played for money, it might have been a different story. Then

Chance said yawning, "Morning will come early and we have to lite out early if we are going to get them steers to Thunder Hawk, so let's call it a night." He added, "Bob, there's a couple of bunk beds in that little room in the barn. You can use one of them. Arora has the only extra bed we have in the house."

Arora lit a lantern. "I'll show you to the bed in the barn." My faithful guide to the barn decided that she might have had too many shots of moonshine to make it back to the house alone, so she just had to lay down with me in the barn, blowing out the lantern as she did. We had some catching up to do with what we had been doing with our lives, and we talked some too. She was a cousin to Kitty and Lora Duncan and a few years younger with fire red hair, independent as a hog on ice, with looks enough to catch the attention of most men. We got to telling about some of our runs out of Canada with whiskey, coming back across North Dakota and nearly getting caught. There weren't many bridges across the Missouri River in North Dakota and you had to cross that river somewhere to get back to the Standing Rock Reservation from Canada, but once back on the reservation, it was clear sailing. The Prohibition agents really concentrated on the river bridges as cars didn't swim well. To avoid getting caught, we needed to figure out a way to bypass the bridges. That was simple enough. We would just drive our load straight south of Canada to the east side of the river across from Fort Yates and then load our whiskey in a canoe and paddle across the river.

Another short night on the home front. When I woke alone, it was already getting light outside. Arora came back in saying, "Good morning sleepy head. I already grained the horses, and it's time to head to the house for breakfast. Come on, we have to slap leather in a little, if we're going to make it to Thunder Hawk by tonight with the herd."

The steers headed out in a hurry. It was harder holding them to a fast walk than it was to get them to go. They went a lot faster than a herd of heavy pregnant cows. The day was good for trailing too, rather cold with a brisk northwest wind; so none of the steers got hot, and we were at John O'Donnell's by midday. John was waiting for us with his bunch of steers; so after a quick lunch at his house, we headed on with all the steers for Thunder Hawk and had them there a little before dark. Herb Lyman with his boys, Jimmy and Tom, along with Jim's help, had their cattle already in the yards at Thunder Hawk. Mother rousted us out early and had us fed with a big breakfast, and then we went at the chore of loading cattle into the boxcars.

We managed to get the train cars all loaded before noon, and we were all assigned a boxcar of steers to ride along with and do the cowpoking. The train slowly left Thunder Hawk, heading east for Sioux City, Iowa. It was a dang cold ride; the boxcars had about a three-inch crack between each board, so the cattle had plenty of air, but insulation, there was none. The steers kept trying to lay down so that helped a little at staying warm, with making like a monkey with a long pole, and climbing along the inside of the boxcar above the steers and poking them up. It wasn't my idea of fun, but it needed doing. The main trick was not to slip or fall down because that could get a person stepped on in a fast hurry. A story that was told of a fellow who'd fallen to that fate stuck vividly in my mind. They found him trampled to death when the cattle were unloaded.

It was near about morning when we rolled to a stop at the Sioux City stockyards. We all survived the trip and didn't lose any steers but were a stinky, sorry looking lot. We found a place to eat right away and then went back to help unload and sort steers, but the stockyard crew already had them unloaded and in pens with feed and water. As we walked into the office at the stockyards, a fellow came at us and introduced himself as Dean Koepnick. As he shook hands with Herb Lyman, he said, "I want to buy all of the steers that you people brought. I'll pay you top dollar, twenty-five dollars for the two's and twenty dollars for the yearlings."

Without hesitation, Herb replied, "Mr. Koepnick, I think you just bought yourself some steers, but some belong to these other folks, so let me talk a minute with them."

John O'Donnell spoke first with, "Sounds like a good price to me," and the rest of us just nodded in agreement. That sure took a lot of sorting out of the picture. I had visualized sorting every steer by brand for ownership, which would have taken up the better part of the day. John dug out his list of owners, and Arora did too.

Koepnick started writing bank drafts, which didn't take him long. Then he asked, "Would any of you be willing to help trail these steers over to my place? It's over near Archer, Iowa, about sixty miles from here. I think we can trail them over there in two days. Going farm wage is fifty dollars a month and keep, but I will pay you five dollars a day starting today, put you up in a hotel for the night, and we'll start the drive first light in the morning. I've bought plenty of saddle horses here. I just don't have enough help that can ride a horse, and I know you cowpokes know how to ride.

"Does that include a woman cowpoke too?" Arora asked.

Dean was quick to answer her, "Hell yes." Then with a smile, "You look like you might even outride some of the fellows here."

Herb declined, "Thanks but no thanks. I need to get my boys and myself back. We have a lot of work to get done before it starts snowing back home."

"I can use the money, so I'm in," offered John O'Donnell. Chance and Arora nodded yes.

Jim and I could use the money, so I spoke for us both, "Why not? We've never trailed cattle in Iowa before, so it'll be a new experience for us."

Dean had hauled four saddled horses over with his Model T truck that had high side boards on it. His neighbor, Jack Lode, had brought four horses in his truck too, so he did have enough horses. We all hopped in the back of Dean's truck, and he hauled us to a hotel; he went ahead of us and told the clerk to give us each a room. The clerk raised an eyebrow a bit and gave us a look, but he said to sign in and handed us keys. After a hot bath, Dean came knocking on our doors to take us to a restaurant for a big meal on him. Dean took a room at the hotel too and made sure we knew that he would be waking us around four in the morning to get an early start with his steers. A good night's sleep sure felt good, but Dean wasn't wrong about his four in the morning. He had us up and fed and in the saddle about first light, and we were on our way with the steers. Dean had hired two lads from the stockyards to help ride drag and he took the lead, riding at a fast walk.

Arora and I took one side and Chance and John took the other, leaving Jim to ride drag with the farm boys, Joe and Pete. Iowa was sure different than South Dakota. It was really flat, with a road or a trail down every mile; most of the lanes were fenced on both sides, so mostly the side riders just had to ride ahead, keeping steers from going down a section line and then ride ahead again to block the section line at the next mile intersection. There being no hills to slow the steers, they really lit out the first few miles and kept us busy riding ahead. Dean's saddle horses left a lot to be desired. They were well enough broke but had the speed of a work horse; my guess would be that's what they were. About all of the land was farmed too, but the corn and wheat had already been harvested; so where there wasn't a fence, it wasn't a problem. It was a cool, cloudy day, and the steers were anxious to travel; we had made it near about fifteen miles in the first four hours, but then the steers slowed down the pace and we went along at a steady pace of close to two and a half miles an hour, which was more to par for trailing cattle. I had my doubts about Dean's statement about making the drive in two days, but when we shoved the last steer into a feed lot a little after sundown, we had traveled thirty-five miles. Dean knew the owner of the lot; Jake and Martha Barren were old friends of his. We put the horses up in the barn, and after a hearty meal at the house, Arora got their spare bedroom and the rest of us made blanket beds on the living room floor and called it a night.

The steers had been on feed and water all night and seemed ready to hit the trail about ten minutes past daylight when we headed them out the gate in the direction of Archer. It was a bit frosty that morning and another good day to trail steers. Dean said we would push them hard and he thought we would make it to his place for supper. I thought that we might be eating a midnight supper. Dean was right; we did make it to his place along about six that evening. As we went across a railroad track at Archer, it occurred to me that Dean could have shipped the steers right over to Archer. When we had the steers in his corral, I asked him, "Why didn't you just ship the steers?"

"Money, my friend. It's a lot cheaper to hire a crew to drive the steers than ship by rail for a short distance," he replied with a grin. The Koepnicks treated us well. Jane Koepnick did a good job at cooking and served wine with the evening meal. She even had beds made up for all of us to sleep in. Dean paid us in cash and took us to the station at six the next morning to catch a train heading west. He didn't have to, but he even paid our train fare back to Thunder Hawk. I, for one, was glad to be out of the saddle again. I liked riding, but it had been a while since I had spent so much time in the saddle, and I had a few places that were a bit sore. It was a long train ride home, and, as we went putting along, I got to thinking maybe I didn't want to be a cowpoke anymore!

CHAPTER 17

Riding the Rails with Uncle John

Uncle John McEldery had always been a favorite of mine, but to most of the family he was a *toki* (tramp). He was Mother's only brother and probably Granddad and Grandmother's only child together. Mother and her sisters had been adopted by Sam McEldery when he married Grandmother Elizabeth. John was always a bit of odd one who turned up after being away for months at a time wearing dirty, tattered old clothes. Once Mother burned all his clothes in the trash barrel and dosed his hair with kerosene to get rid of the fleas before she'd let him in the house. After he'd get scrubbed up and into some of Dad's old clothes, he would start telling us kids all the places he'd seen. Some sounded fascinatin' and some sounded just downright dangerous. Uncle John had a way with telling a story. He had some schooling and had read probably more books than our town library held. After roaming, he'd rest up with us or one of his other sisters, maybe doing some odd jobs for a little money, and when he was ready, he'd hop the rails and move on, never writing even a postcard. Eventually our family just accepted that it was Uncle John's way and stopped worrying about him. Some said it was his way of being a nomad, a wanderer, a *nuniyan wiscasa* (wandering man).

Since it seemed like a good idea to be out of town for a while after the incident in Deadwood, I took up Uncle John's offer to ride the rails with him for a time. No tickets, no cops, no one knowing where I was headed had some value just then. We had covered hundreds of miles going from boxcar to boxcar on different trains but always we were heading west. Lots of men and boys were hopping freight trains in those days to get somewhere with a better chance of finding a job, to visit family, or just to see the world. We had joined up with some other "sidecar Pullman" travelers at a hobo camp and were thinking a hot dinner would sure taste good after so many miles. We had hiked into a middling town somewhere in Nevada in search of some groceries. In my mind I was going back to days when Brave Bear and I traveled on horseback across Montana and South Dakota and joined up with Bill Cody's Wild West show when Uncle John's high but scratchy voice brought me back to the present.

"Ever have hobo stew?" he inquired.

"Never even heard of it," I replied.

"Well then, let's grab a ham and some biscuits," he said as he opened the door to a grocery store in the dry and dusty but bustling town. "When we get on back to camp, you will be in for a surprise with supper this evening."

I still had a little money from my trip to Iowa, so I paid for the vittles. Back at camp, Uncle John handed our contribution to the evening meal to the man in charge of the stew pot, a fellow going by the name of Dub Dawson. I took a quick gander over in the direction of my bedroll; it was just where I had left it, so maybe Uncle was some right about there being honor among thieves. This hobo jungle camp was sure a far cry from any camp I had ever been in. Most of the guys hadn't cleaned up in the least in a very long time. Kind of a sorry-looking bunch. Most of the fellows were just lying around, so I stretched out on my bedroll.

"Don't be too harsh about judging these boys," said Uncle John recognizing the look on my face as a questioning one. "Some come from wealthy families and some are well educated gents, but they're all just down on their luck." Uncle lowered his voice as he sat down by me, "Take Dub there, he was a bank president down in Kansas, but when his bank closed, he lost all of his own money, too. Then to add frosting to the cake, when he told his wife he had lost his job and all their money, she ran him out of their house with a shotgun. His so-called friends were only fair-weather friends, not a one would loan him a dollar or a bed to sleep in, so he left town in a boxcar and turned to being a hobo." Pointing to a fellow a ways over wearing a black tuxedo suit that had seen better days, he said, "He's called Ichabod Crane—probably just his hobo name as most here don't use their real names. Story has it that he was a school teacher for many years, then a toughie sparking his gal, beat him bad and ran him out of town. Anyway, we Indians always walk a mile in the other fellow's shoes, right Bobbie Boy."

"Sure," I answered, but no one had called me Bobbie in many a moon.

"All the fellows here have different stories, mostly sad, in their life that led them here. Now I suppose you're wondering about my story too. Well, sit back and I will tell you a little of why I am a hobo. Back when I was still a boy—I had just turned eighteen—Dad wanted me to join the army; he said that it'd make a man out of me. But Mother had other ideas for her only son—she thought I should go on to school and become somebody important—a lawyer or a doctor. I just couldn't decide what to do. I had been seeing this pretty Indian gal *Skoo-yah* (Sweet Brown Otter). Her father got in with the Bureau of Indian Affairs and had a good-paying job, so they had money and a nice home. Some of the kids we had gone to school with were so poor that some came to school without shoes and some had holes in their clothes. I always had good clothes and plenty to eat, and I looked down on all those poor kids and said mean things to them. I was just a dumb, naive, spoiled kid, and I never even thought about walking a mile in their shoes, suppose because they didn't have shoes.

"At any rate, I was head over heels in love with Skoo-yah and she with me, but we couldn't decide what to do. We wanted to get married and raise a family, but how was the problem. I supposed I could try farming and raise cattle, but I knew in my heart that

I wouldn't be much good as a farmer and I didn't even like cows. Skoo-yah came up with a plan: we would go pray in the old Indian way and hope for a vision to tell us what to do. We had both gone to Indian boarding schools where they washed our mouths out with soap if we even brought up such ideas, but we had listened to our grandmothers and other elders and we knew something of the old ways.

"We first had to do a sweat ceremony to purify ourselves. Sweats were part of the Indian religion that whites didn't want Indians to practice anymore as they thought they were just primitive superstition. The *teh-m'ne te-pe* or sweat lodge was made of a circle of tree branches, with the tops bent over and tied together forming a low room, then hides covered over the branches making the enclosure completely dark. A buffalo skull was placed in the lodge as an altar, a center for focusing one's thoughts. One person would tend a fire just outside of the lodge for hours to heat stones. When they were ready, the hot stones were placed around the alter. Then the people who wanted to attend the sweat ceremony would sit in the sweat lodge and meditate on whatever was on their minds as the tender would drip water on the hot stones causing much steam. It would be quite hot with steam in the sweat lodge. After a person meditated and prayed enough, that person would leave the sweat and go out and wash off in a nearby stream.

"After we had did the sweat, that afternoon Skoo-yah and I walked up to the top of a high hill just to the west of Fort Yates to have our visions. We sat on that hill all afternoon and nothing. It was way into the night, really dark, then suddenly the sky came to light. We could see just as plain as day a white eagle came flying from the clouds along with this white buffalo. They both stopped out from us maybe twenty feet. They were just standing in the air, the eagle had black shiny eyes with black feet, and the buffalo also had black eyes that sparkled, black hoofs that shined, with a few black hairs on its knees and chin, other that they were snow white. The eagle spoke to Skoo-yah, saying, 'I will tell you what you have asked,' but the voice was coming from Skoo-yah, only it was like she was coming out of the back of the eagle and just visible from the waist up and that Skoo-yah was talking to her. Then the eagle talking through her said, 'You are a leader of your people; your people need you. This man with you knows only greedy ways; he is not for you.'

"Then my image came up from the buffalo; I seemed to be standing in the buffalo, just behind his hump, and I spoke then, back to myself, saying, 'You must leave here and go out into the world and make amends for your ways with the very poorest of this land. The white owl will carry your spirit to the spirit world in pieces if you stay. Do this, and you will find happiness.' Then our images disappeared, and the eagle and the buffalo turned and went back into the clouds with darkness coming back around us in full force. Skoo-yah and I were mighty scared as we ran off that hill. When we were back at Skoo-yah's door, she gave me a kiss, whispering, 'I will not kiss you ever again. You must go, and we must do as our visions spoke.' This is a story I thought you would want to know. I never told it to anyone else. It is my story, so now you know why I am a hobo. Maybe it was just a dream or superstition, but I choose to believe it."

It was already dark when Dub hollered out, "Stew's ready!" I was a little more than dubious to try his hobo stew but to my surprise, it was without a doubt, the best stew I had ever eaten.

I couldn't help but compliment the cook, "Best stew I've ever had. You should be a cook in a fancy restaurant!"

"Thank you," he replied. "I have been giving that some thought. I like cooking. I used to cook at home all the time, but my parents pushed me into doing something as they would say 'more proper,' but, yes, I think now it's time for me to do what I want."

Uncle John was quick to pick up on Dub's spark of hope and said, "Dub, you are dang good at cooking and wasting your time cooking for us hobos. I seen a 'cook wanted' sign in the window of a café up town. In the morning, let's get you sparked up and see what you can do."

Dub weakly nodded in the right direction and then said, "Okay, but if I have to bathe in the Truckee River, then all you guys are coming too." The river was only a stone's throw from our camp. In a short minute, there were fifteen of us striping naked on the river bank. That river was a might cold, like jumping into a tub of ice water only a lot deeper. The Truckee did suffice; we all took a very fast bath. Early the next morning, I gave Dub my extra change of clothes, and we were off to work, for Dub anyway. Uncle John and I went with Dub; the other fellows mostly were still sleeping when we left camp. We walked into a busy café; one fellow behind the counter seemed to be the boss. Dub slowly walked over to the gent; I thought he was going to get cold feet, but Dub managed to stammer out, "I can cook a little. Do you still need a cook?"

The man behind the counter threw Dub an apron, saying, "Hell yes, let's see what you can do!"

Dub went a-zipping back to the kitchen, and Uncle John and I took a booth and ordered breakfast. Someone cooked us a good breakfast; likely it was Dub. As I paid for our meal, the gent behind the counter said, "Looks like I got me a cook. Thanks for bringing him in. I'll take good care of him; a cook's hard to find in these parts."

After we got back to the camp, Uncle said, "Doesn't look like we have anything to hold us here. Let's hop the next train heading toward San Francisco." I started to roll up my blanket, but I seen a young-looking kid lying in the grass trying to cover himself with weeds, so I spread my blanket over him, without even saying a word. And we were off to a curve in the track where the train had to slow so we could easily hop on.

We were off the train and hiding from train inspectors about as much as we were riding the train, and I started to thinking that maybe riding the rail wasn't as glamorous as I had been led to believe by a certain uncle of mine. I never gave it much thought as to what trains hauled before, but now I was seeing it firsthand. I was about to hop in an empty car just behind one that had crates stacked high full of turkeys, but Uncle John put his hand on my arm. "Never get right behind a car of chickens, turkeys, or pigs— they stink too much, and don't hop in one that has been hauling coal." The weather had been warm for fall, but today sitting in a boxcar turned into a dang cold ride in nothing flat, especially coming over the Sierras. Uncle found some newspapers, and we wrapped them around us and covered ourselves with some paper boxes. It helped but it was still not so comfortable. After a few brief stops to eat and many long hours of bouncing along on slow trains, we finally hopped off before we got to the Union Pacific's depot to stay a bit in San Francisco.

It was much warmer even with the fog coming off the bay; we mostly didn't even need a coat. The hobos in the yard there greeted Uncle John like an old friend. It was dark when we arrived, but by all the lights in different places I surmised that we were in a pretty big town and hilly country. I was really tired after the long rail riding, so after a few introductions, I nudged my traveling companion, whispering, "Let's just get a room at a hotel. I'll pay for it."

"That won't be necessary. Come along," he said with a slow grin. As we were hoofing it across those up and down hills into San Francisco, Uncle said, "I have a lady friend here; she will put us up for the night." That took me by surprise. I hadn't thought of Uncle as a ladies' man. I hadn't even seen him give any women along the way a second look.

"This woman is really a special gal. I always stay with her when I'm not hoboing. Her name is Hu-Li Chan, but I call her Molly. She has a baby sister, Zhang, sharing her house, but I think they'll let you sleep on their couch. There is something more I will tell you about, part of my 'story,' but it has to stay under your hat. You cannot tell family or anyone."

I assured him. "You can trust me not to tell your secret, whatever it is."

"I work for some federal boys as an informant. This hobo run is just a way for me to case the hobo jungles for wanted criminals, rapists, murderers, and just really bad guys. We don't bother with chicken thieves, bootleggers, and such. Felons on the run often go hide and hang out in these hobo jungles. When I spot a known criminal character, I go to the next town and send a wire to the feds and they do the rest. I've given up quite a few bad guys over the years. There would be an awful payback if they knew I was the one responsible for their getting caught, plus it would shoot the hell out of my cover. So keep it quiet."

"Uncle, I had no idea, but I most certainly will keep a lid on it."

"I was sent back to the Dakotas to try to get a handle on a Prohibition agent roaming that area, goes by Two-Gun Heart.

Rumor has it that he takes a big payoff to let booze move around in that area, but he's a slick operator and hard to catch with any proof. The boys I work for don't care about a little booze slipping through, but they have reason to believe that this Two-Gun character may have somehow been involved in the mysterious death of a bootlegger back in Nebraska."

I was taken aback a little, and replied, "I know a little of this Two-Gun Heart. People say he is part Indian or Mexican, but I don't think so. He stopped me a couple of times and searched my outfit for booze. I ditched my hooch before he stopped me, but the last time we met, he told me that I was on his 'list,' so I made a lot of effort to avoid meeting up with him. He sounded more like the boys in Chicago than any Indian I ever knew. I do believe he is something other than what he seems to be."

We had made it to a section of San Francisco with streetlights, but it didn't look like the best part of town. The buildings were low and on the shabby side. The people we had met walking along didn't look to be too prosperous.

As he saw my uneasiness, Uncle said, "We're in Chinatown now. The Chinese are very poor here. Mostly they came over here with the promise of getting rich in the gold fields but found that the gold rush had run out and they didn't have money to go back to China. They take any work they can find, mostly the hard jobs others don't want. Molly and Zhang came with their parents from China, but their mother died on the boat and their father worked very hard picking fruit and vegetables to support them—the girls worked in the fields as well. Mr. Chan died a few years back. When I first came out this way, I took a job, working undercover for the Fed boys, picking berries just south of San Jose. That's how I met Mr. Chan and his daughters Hu-Li and Zhang working in the strawberry fields. There had been a rapist in that area attacking and killing young women; the feds wanted me to help with catching the scum. I was supposed to just let them know if I suspected anyone. Well, it didn't quite work that way.

"There were a lot of people picking berries, including me, although I'm not much of a berry picker. We had been stooping over rows of berries all day; it was almost dusk when I heard a whimpering coming from behind some bushes. I took a quick look-see to find a white butt of a fellow showing; he was on top of a Chinese gal, and she was struggling and whimpering, but he had a knife against her throat. I didn't think about the feds; I just hit him across the back of his head with my bucket of berries and grabbed the knife from his hand, then rolled him on his back, holding his knife against his throat. My plan was to detain him until someone could get the police, but the fellow tried getting up fast, and his knife cut his throat a little; then he started bleeding quite a bit, but he didn't get up. The feds just kept a low profile keeping still on that one, but the local police said I had done them a great favor and that it was clearly self-defense, so they didn't charge me with anything. They even gave me some reward money; plus it didn't blow my cover. The Chinese gal was Zhang; her father and Hu-Li were so thankful that I had to just go home with them that night. I started calling Hu-Li Molly because I thought 'Who Lie' sounded a bit odd, and she said she didn't mind if I called her Molly. That night I got the best massage from the prettiest little Chinese gal, Molly, and we've been together since that night. I love her like no other and I'm sure she feels the same toward me."

Uncle John pointed to a nice looking house, one of the better ones in this area, and said, "There it is, our home. I paid for it but put Molly's name on the title." We didn't even knock; Uncle just walked in to the surprise of a couple of Chinese women, but they were both right quick to greet Uncle with hugs. Then they noticed me. Uncle turned to me and introduced me to Molly, then Zhang. "Here is my nephew, Bob, from Thunder Hawk, South Dakota. I brought him back with me to show him this country." Molly was pretty; it was easy to see why Uncle was attracted to her. She looked close to middle aged, not a lot younger than Uncle, and Zhang looked some younger—I thought maybe in her midthirties and just as pretty as a picture, but about as small as a bug's ear.

"I don't know about you, but I'm for having a quick shower and shave and taking these lovely ladies out to dinner." They had running water inside, with even hot water, really modern. I didn't need to be told twice. I was way past the tad side of hungry and felt more than some stinky, so it was a fast cleanup, with Uncle lending me a clean set of his clothes. He had more fancy duds than I would have ever suspected. Who would have thought that of Uncle John? He always came back our way looking like a hobo, broke, grubby, and clothes that had seen better days.

I had never had much in the area of Chinese food, just what Sammy Wong cooked back home, but he didn't cook much in the way of Chinese. The ladies prettied up too, not that they weren't already pretty, but they put on long silk dresses with bright flowers stitched on them. Then we were off to Uncle's favorite Chinese restaurant, and as soon as we walked, in we were warmly greeted, and the chief cook came out and shook Uncle's hand. I took it from our royal welcome that my uncle was known and liked by all the Chinese, at least those in the restaurant. I had to try many different foods—they were all good, and I was as full as a tick by the time I had sampled them all. As we were leaving, Uncle said, "I'll get this one; you've been buying me meals all the way from Thunder Hawk." But Molly paid for our meals—I reckon the money came from the same pocket. It was getting on the order of late evening now, and I was really tired, so it was back to their house and sleep on the couch for me. Uncle and Molly headed for their bedroom, saying good night, leaving me alone with Zhang. "Zhang, if you have a spare blanket, I'll just stretch out on your couch," I offered.

"You take my bed; guests here don't sleep on the couch." She showed me to her bed and how to get in it, not that I couldn't find my way into a bed. That Zhang sure had a comfortable bed; I didn't even snore, and I must have slept a good share of the night, anyway. But morning came with Uncle tapping on the bedroom door.

I spent the better part of a week with Uncle and his fantastic ladies; they sure showed me the sights of San Francisco. Think I could have just stayed with them forever. I got to thinking about my obligations back home and what Tubby would say if I weren't there to do my part. Moreover, I didn't want to wear out my welcome here either, and not having a job might just run my money supply completely short. I would either have to get a job here or go home, so I told Uncle John I would have to be going back to Thunder Hawk.

"I expected you would be heading back. I will see you when I am back that way again, more than likely in spring. The feds still want me to do some checking on that Two-Gun fellow."

Uncle shook my hand, Molly gave me a hug at the train station, but Zhang gave me a long kiss good-bye; then I paid the fare and hopped on the passenger train heading in the direction of Thunder Hawk. I had had enough of that hobo life, and it was getting too cold to be sitting in a boxcar for two thousand miles. I had plenty of time to think on the way back home, but I kept wondering if Uncle's story about the vision was true or if it was just his imagination. It did get him off the reservation and started on a rather interesting life. If he believed it, then it was true to him anyway. He may have just had a bad dream. But if there was just one God and he made all humankind, then why couldn't he have given the Indians a prophet or prophets over the years or some form of guidance like a vision? Seems odd to me that he would give others guidance and totally ignore the Indians. Maybe, just maybe, others called Indians savages because of ignorance. I thought, "Whatever a person believes matter less than if they believe it with all their heart. If they do, it would be right for them."

My run on the rails with my uncle sure gave me a much higher level of respect for him. And it taught me to keep looking beyond the surface of things, and people.

CHAPTER 18

Blind Man's Bluff

When I got back, I found that things had been going pretty well at the moonshine operation. In fact, probably too well. Tubby and Dwight had built up quite a lot of inventory. They had expanded the moonshine output and had a lot of the product on hand.

Maybe Dad had seen the future when moonshining wouldn't be so profitable anymore. He'd had quite a few talks with Tubby and Dwight over penny-ante cards and told them that pig raising was going to be the way to make money from now on. The government was even helping farmers pay for their first pigs. A pig would eat anything, anything at all. It seemed like odd advice from the aging frontiersman, but Tubby listened with interest. "You don't have to have much land for them; they eat the stuff that cows wouldn't touch, and you don't have to trail them. Forget those sheep that the Duncans are raising. They won't pay their way. They make too damn much noise with all that bleating, and you've got to have a good herding dog to work sheep. Pigs, that's the way to go."

Well, Tubby and Dwight were never ones to look past a way to make money without too much work, and moonshine didn't make itself. You had to be careful and get the proportions just right and keep the equipment clean. Everybody in the area knew that Danny Williams drank some bad hooch and it left him with a permanent shaking condition. Must have messed up his nervous system bad. Danny didn't clean his tubing and look what happened to him. He got the shakes so bad he couldn't button his pants.

So Tubby took Dad's advice and ordered a bunch of registered Yorkshire hogs shipped in from Iowa. He set up troughs and watering tanks and thought of all the money he would make without having to ride a horse or pull a hay wagon. Dad even got a few hogs for the homeplace for Jim to tend.

Most of the latest batch of moonshine was ready to put into quart and pint bottles for distributing, but coming up right behind was another batch of fermented mash in barrels. My little escapade in Deadwood had kind of put a damper on things, and Tubby and Dwight began some sniping at each other. Just as Dwight was saying to Tubby, "If you're such a goddamn genius, you just make it all yourself..." when a haze of dust on the section line road told them that a car was headed toward the farm at reckless speed.

"What in tarnation?" asked Tubby.

No sooner had Todd Kruze climbed out of his roadster than he started rattling off as fast as he could, "The revenuers are coming, the revenuers are coming! They got word of the still and they are on the way. They were tipped off. It must have that sumbitch, Rudolf Kunnouf, he wanted to run moonshine for me a few days back. It felt like he would be a snitch and I turned him down on his offer."

"We will work later on who tipped them off, but right now we've got to get rid of the booze and the mash, too," said Tubby calmly.

Bessie came out of the house just then, hushed the girls back into the house, and told them in no uncertain terms to stay there. There was work to be done.

"There's no time for talk. Tubby, most of the mason jars in the cellar are clean and sterile for this year's canning. You can pour as much moonshine into them as they will hold. Fill them all the way to top and screw on the lids. Push them behind the pickles and jam, and they'll just look like empty jars on the shelves down in the dark root cellar.

"Dwight, you take those barrels of mash and pour them out in the pig pen. That'll hide the stink and the revenuers sure won't go in there. Todd you take a hammer and nails and nail that panel in the well up tight, and start a big fire in the forge."

The boys hustled up to follow Bessie's orders. By the time they'd finished, they could see two big clouds of dust coming down the road from the direction of Lemmon. Bessie had tied on a fresh apron and put on a pot of coffee, Dwight was pounding away with hammer and tongs at the forge, Tubby was up in the pig shed shoveling manure, and Todd was putting his tools away. When the cars roared up into the driveway, Bessie was pounding away on the piano, "Onward Christian Soldiers," with a vigor she usually reserved for beating rugs.

Two cars pulled up and a bunch of revenuers jumped out and came up to the door.

"US Prohibition agents. Open up! We got a warrant to search the premises. You can't hide your goddamn still here any longer," shouted Two-Gun Hart. He was all dressed up in his "cowboy" outfit with shaggy fur chaps, a ten-gallon Stetson, snakeskin boots, and a pistol holster on each hip. Two-Gun's idea of what a cowboy looked like was pretty much from the last century when there was still open range. The rest of the agents had on dark suits and shiny city shoes. Working ranchers usually had more practical clothes and our boots were usually a little down at the heel from working cattle. Dakota farmers like Tubby and Dwight dressed somewhere in between farmer style with overalls and cowboy style with a Stetson or straw cowboy hat in the summer. Dad had told that he would never hire a man wearing lace-up boots or a straw hat, because if they weren't lacing their boots, they were chasing after their straw hat! But, not everyone felt things his way.

"Sir," said Bessie with her hands on her hips, "there are children here. Watch your language! Now you just show me that warrant, and then maybe we'll show you around."

He backed off about three steps from the door and waved the warrant at Bessie. "Beggin' your pardon, ma'am. We didn't expect to find you here."

She read the warrant and it was legal all right, so she said, "Look around gentlemen. All you'll find here is a hardworking farm with hardworking farmers. We raise wheat and rye, and pigs. Do you like pigs? We have about thirty pigs. The best Yorkshire hogs around these parts, brought from the stockyards in Sioux City."

Two-Gun sent his men up down and all around the farmstead. There were quite a few buildings for them to search besides the house, half a dozen granaries, the cattle barn, the pig shed, the forge, and the root cellar. It took a while since they were all city boys and didn't know where to look.

One of them found a piece copper tubing at the forge, and exclaimed, "What's this for? Watering your hogs?"

"Why yes," said Dwight with a grin. "I thought you government agents knew all about the latest hog-farming techniques. We're using it to run water right from the windmill into the hog's troughs. Do you want to see how it works?"

"No. Guess pigs gotta drink," he stammered in a deep slightly thick sounding voice that I remembered from the boys back in Chicago. They seemed to get confused with between t's and d's.

The agents ransacked, looked up and down, over and under, even lowered a bucket into the well, but found nothing. They glanced at the "empty" mason jars in the cellar and sidled back to Two-Gun looking kinda of hangdog.

"We didn't find nothin', boss. It's clean here. Nothin' but some empty barrels in da barn."

"Let's get out of here," Hart sputtered. "I didn't get youse this time, but don't worry. Youse half-breeds are on my outlaw list and I will get youse. I always get da ones who don't play ball our way. Da ones who don't know how to pony-up, but dey should learn, if dey wanna stay in business." I heard that confusion between *t*'s and *d*'s in his voice, too, again reminding me of the boys in Chicago. In Lakota, the difference between a *t* and *d* can change the meaning of what you say, guess not in Chicago. We had heard talk about the "pony-up" with Hart but tended to ignore it. There were others who were eager to pony-up for him to look the other way when they were running moonshine. Hart and his boys all got back into their cars and drove out as fast as they came, leaving more dust behind.

"Come on in the kitchen," Bessie said to the men. "We can drink this coffee while it's still hot. Girls, you can go on back outside and play till it starts getting dark."

Just as they were beginning to talk over the day's events and what they might mean, their oldest girl Ethel came running into the house. "Momma, Daddy, come see the pigs dancing. They are up on their hind legs doing all kinds of twist and turns. I never seen pigs dancing before. They are dancing and rolling over and over," she cried with delight. "You've got to see."

"You never 'saw' pigs dancing before," corrected Bessie. "And you won't see them again." And they all went out to the pigpen to see the wondrous sight.

These events got me to thinking that maybe my days hauling and just slipping past the revenuers' snares might be getting a little short. A gambler once told me the trick to being a winner is to quit when you are ahead.

Although I was still making more money running moonshine than I did with cattle, I had begun to start up a regular herd of my own again. Jim was home with the folks, and he could handle our little bunch of cattle. Dad was always finding him extra little jobs trying to keep him out of mischief, but Jim had a knack for getting into trouble anyway. It was getting into hard winter by the time we sold out of moonshine. Two-Gun and his henchmen had made several raids on stills all over North Dakota and South Dakota and busted several of our steady suppliers. Danny Williams had nearly died from drinking his own moonshine. It poisoned him and left him with nerves so bad that so he shook all the time. After his story got around, some folks were hesitant in a big way about buying moonshine, but whiskey was still a big seller.

Arora and I took a run to Canada; she followed me with her car and we didn't have any trouble with the border patrol or revenuers, but we drove in a snowstorm on our tail, most of the way back to the east side of the river across from Fort Yates. The river was froze and some were even driving across, but we weren't that brave or foolish. Snooky Goodreau and Chip McLaughlin met us at the river with a team and sled. They didn't break through the ice with their team, but a team is a lot lighter than a car. Then we drove around back to Fort Yates and gathered up our whiskey; we left Chip and Snooky with a good supply of whiskey for their troubles as they were our bootleggers for the Fort Yates area. We hadn't anticipated a snowstorm, but, in North Dakota, snowstorms are quite frequent. And the snow just kept piling up that winter.

I told Arora that I didn't think we should make any more winter runs to Canada, and she was quick to agree. My roadster was fast on dry roads, but it sure wasn't much good in snow. I decided to leave it parked in the barn for a spell and took a job helping a friend, Avery Clarkson, with hauling hay to his cattle. He had a fair-size herd of cattle, and he had been sickly all fall and didn't get all of his hay hauled to the place. I only figured to help him a few weeks but it turned into a few months job. Feeding cows is an everyday job in the winter, especially when the snow gets deep like it did that year. Each day we would each drive a team with sled and hay rack out to the hay stack, pitch on a load, haul it to the cows, and then pitch it off.

Spring finally came, and I went back to trying to deliver booze from Canada. Tubby had gone out of the moonshine business after the visit from Two-Gun, but he was glad to see me. He told me that Arora wasn't running shine any more. She had met a fellow who worked on the railroad, and they had gotten married a couple of months back. I had not expected that. I stammered on that one but was finally able to speak, "She must have got tired of waiting on me to get rich. We had talked about getting together after we had enough money saved up but now looks like it was just a one-sided idea."

"Well, life is like that. You wait too long and all the good ones get snatched up, but as the saying goes, there are a lot of fish in the sea," said Tubby trying to take the sting out a little.

"That's true I suppose, but I think if you want to catch fish, you have to go where the fish are," I said.

"There's going to be a dance in Thunder Hawk Saturday night, might be a place to start 'fishing,'" Tubby replied.

Dad had been feeling poorly, so he didn't come to the dance to play his fiddle, but Abe was there with Viola and Jim came along too. There were others around who could play music for a dance, and did. A large crowd was already gathered at the hall and music was already playing, but I had several requests for some hooch and had to oblige several of the fellows before I made my way into the dance hall.

The Williamson clan were the first I recognized. Their folks had a homestead some twenty miles north of Thunder Hawk, in the Pretty Rock hills. It was mostly a rock farm and there were over a dozen kids in their family, so wealthy was not in their league. Earl came over introducing me to his wife Lulea and four of his sisters who were with him as well: Betty, Blanch, Carrie, and Susan. I knew the girls from previous dances—especially Betty—and I had met his brothers Chancey, Buck, and Kack before as well. Earl wanted to know if I by chance had anything to liven up the boys. As I went to dance with Betty, I told him that he might find a jug of moonshine under the seat of my car if he wanted to limber up the boys so they could dance. Abe and Jim were quick to join Earl and the other boys out by the car.

Betty and I danced several dances, and I kinda lost track of the others enjoying her company. When Earl and his brothers came back in, Kack went over to the band and started singing an old cowboy ballad, "The Strawberry Roan" and then he picked up "Little Joe the Wrangler." His singing was a little off key, but he didn't miss a word. The crowd gave him a big hand and shouted for him to sing another one! Kack sang "Little Brown Jug," after that one, we went back to dancing, but he did some kind of a jig by himself. Betty said that Kack never even sang at home, so he must have sipped too much spirit water, but Earl assured us that they only had a couple of drinks. Kack was enjoying himself, and he did liven up the crowd.

As Betty and I were dancing, she told me that she had given up on John Ellison; he was supposed to take her to this dance but didn't show. They had been engaged for four years but now she thought John had cold feet or just changed his mind, so I offered to take her home, and she accepted my offer. I left my brothers to find their own way.

CHAPTER 19

Dead Man's Hand

Meeting Betty at that dance was one of the best things that ever happened to me, but for Jim and Abe, things just seemed to go more out of control. When I got back from a run over to the Eagle Butte area, Dad told me that both my brothers had been arrested on a charge of assault. It seems that they got into a fight with John Nelson in the pool hall in Thunder Hawk. Dad read aloud from the *Lemmon Leader* newspaper:

> The Gilland boys had attended a dance at Thunder Hawk the night before and were not in the best spirits, coupled with the fact John Nelson had made some false accusations concerning them. Nelson lost a set of harnesses a couple of weeks ago and he insinuated that the Gilland boys took them, and when they met Nelson Sunday they had their fighting clothes on.

Dad wasn't there, so he didn't see what happened, but the paper went on to say:

> Jim was going to make Nelson take back everything he said and swung a healthy right to Nelson's mouth, but Nelson came back for more, and it was apparent that Jim had taken in

too much territory. Abe entered the fracas and it was a three-cornered affair for a minute.

Next thing, when Jim got away, he grabbed a billiard ball and threw it at Nelson, striking him just above the temple cutting an artery and fracturing his skull.

"That son of a bitch Nelson had it coming for a long time," Dad sort of wheezed out breathing hard, "but Jim could have just hit again with his right. Bustin' his head with a billiard ball was maybe going too far."

According to the newspaper account, "The fight was over as far as Mr. Nelson was concerned; the birds were singing him a lullaby. He was taken to Lemmon for medical attention."

The birds did sing him to sleep, but he came to in the morning. Both Abe and Jim were brought to McIntosh and lodged in the jail. Abe furnished bond, but Dad refused bail for Jim. He was held on a charge of assault with a dangerous weapon with a possible one- to five-year penitentiary sentence. The part in the paper that worried Dad most, and he was glad Mother couldn't read, said, "There is considerable feeling around Thunder Hawk, and if found guilty, the boys are apt to get a long trip."

Dad wouldn't bail Jim out of jail. "It's time for him to learn something. Jim has been raising hell a lot and in more fights than a fighting cock. I'm through with trying to keep him out of trouble," he said with the saddest voice I'd ever heard him use.

Abe wasn't any better. His and Viola's little girl, Iris, had died from diphtheria that winter. After Iris died, Abe went to partying a bunch more than he should have. When he partied, he was the last of the big spenders, and everyone around him had to have drinks too. Abe and Viola bought a new Ford sedan that spring—the latest model in dark green that could reach forty-five miles per hour in less than a minute—and it seemed to make Abe more cheerful for a while. He drove it at top speed even when he wasn't going anywhere important. I did kind of wonder how he found the money for a brand-new car, but I knew Abe didn't like to talk about such things either. Viola had started teaching again at the Thunder

Hawk school and tried hard to make a life with Abe work, but in my opinion, she was on an uphill run.

We did have more cattle than most in the area, but pasture for the cattle was becoming a concern with homesteaders on a lot of the good land. The land not taken by homesteaders was better land for running cattle on anyway. Homesteaders had to farm at least forty acres of their homestead, which was not near enough land to make them an honest living. Many of the homesteaders were from the cities back east and had no idea about farming or living in the country. Some even had given up good jobs to come west and seek their fortunes with the promise of free land stuck foremost in their minds. The government, and the railroads, wanted the land settled, especially on the reservations, because it was a way, supposedly, to teach the Indians the white-man ways. With neighbors came inter-marriages, too, and that also would decrease any threat of Indian uprising. That's probably why the reservation was opened to home-steading in the first place.

The majority of the homesteaders were very poor to begin with, spending all they ever had just to get out to the Dakotas. When crops failed and food was scarce, many of them hightailed it back east, but some who stayed took to making moonshine or whatever they could do to feed their families. The homesteaders were mostly an honest lot, but desperation causes people to do strange things. The land was free, but there were some clauses that were not well mentioned up front. Taxes were assessed on the land and had to be paid each year; if the taxes weren't paid after four years, the land was taken by the county and sold for the taxes against it. The homesteaders had to prove up on the land by living on it for three consecutive years, farming at least forty acres, and they had to have at least one cow and a plow. Most came with a team and wagon, living out of their wagon until they could stick up some kind of a shanty. In some places, the sod could be cut into layers and stacked like bricks to build a sod house, which at least kept the cold out. But many homesteader shanties were built on sledges in town and dragged to the claim over the snow and ice in winter. These were made of a light wood frame covered with tar paper—one room, one window, and a door. Dakota winters were another thing that many of the homesteaders were not aware of—they had no idea how hard and relentless the winter storms were at times. Tar-paper walls didn't do much to keep winter outside; some never made it through the first winter before they pulled up stakes and left.

With Jim in jail and Dad not well, I needed to stay home at the ranch with the folks and get to the chore of getting some hay made for the coming winter. I felt a bit relieved to go home to real work. After so many whiskey and moonshine runs, I was luckier than most in not ending up caught by the revenuers. I was way overdue to be arrested for running illegal spirits, so yes, it was time to give up that life. And Betty had turned my head and heart hard. I knew she would never accept me if I continued running booze.

Jim and Abe's trial was held in quick time on a hot summer day at the courthouse in McIntosh. Jim received a sentence of two years in hard rock city for his part in the fight with John Nelson. I sure didn't want to hear the word "Leavenworth" in the same breath as my little brother's name, but at least it wasn't maximum sentence. Dad was relieved that it was only two years and said that maybe it would teach Jim the lesson he needed. I guess maybe it did and kept him from worse things, but we didn't yet know that. The charges against Abe were dismissed by the court because he was able to prove that he was trying to get between John Nelson and Jim, and he had not landed a blow to Nelson. After the trial, Nelson told anyone who would listen to him that he would even the score with Abe. Most thought it was as an idle threat. I knew my brothers were not guilty of taking John Nelson's harness because that just wasn't the sort of thing they would do unless it had been a prank, but it was no prank. Jack McGuire had stood up at the trial and told that he knew where John's harness went and that neither Abe nor Jim had anything to do with the harness disappearing, but Nelson still swore he would get his revenge. Jim wasn't charged with stealing the harness, just for hitting Nelson.

Dad turned in his chips not long after Jim was sentenced. He had been in failing health for some time, and it seemed that the trial just took his last bit of strength. He had been having stomach problems for a while. Doc Totten had often been at the house with bottles and pills. He gave Dad something that caused him to pass a five-foot-long tapeworm. For a long time, Doc Totten had been telling Dad to eat right and no more booze of any kind, but, well, with him it was like telling a kid no more candy. He had stomach cancer, and Mother said he knew it, but he just had to go on one more drinking binge—which he did, and it killed him. I reckon he knew his time was short and just decided to end it faster than live longer and become an invalid. Dad didn't go to any kind of church, said his church was on horseback, so we had small funeral at the house with just the family and a few old friends.

Dad had seen a lot of changes in his over fifty years on the reservation, from the tall grass prairie when he first came out and joined the army in 1875, to the coming of the railroads and white settlers. Where tepees stood when he was a young man, there were now towns with brick schools, banks, and hospitals. In his last years, he often drifted back to those earlier days when he and Mother were young. Mother honored Dad's wishes and had a tombstone put up in the cemetery in Lemmon, engraved with the crossed sabers of the US Cavalry and the legend "Winners of the West." Seems a fitting caption for a man of his stature.

After Dad's funeral, I found it easier to get back to hauling in hay rather than sit around mourning, but Abe took the other trail and went to drinking more than before. Abe and Tom Kane had gone up to Morristown to do some repair work on the harvesting machines they used for cutting flax. One night in September with a full moon, he and a few others went into Morristown, drinking and just raising hell.

The Morristown sheriff, Henry Uhrig, tried to arrest Abe for driving recklessly through town and turning that green Ford in circles on the main street. Abe kept on with his wild driving until Sheriff Uhrig, accompanied by Two-Gun Hart, the federal Prohibition agent who was always showing up when there was an Indian to be arrested, ran them out of town with their guns drawn.

Sheriff Uhrig just warned them, "You boys all to go sober up before you get in worse trouble next time."

Hart had a lot more to say that night. "I know about how youse was running booze but not playing ball wid the right people." He shouted, "Youse damn breeds think you can play by your own rules.

Well, that's not going to go on much longer." But like a lot of words coming out of Hart's mouth, it was sort of mumbled and hard to understand—his *t*'s and *d*'s all mixed up.

Abe and the Kane boys, Tom and Victor, and Frank Hourigan drove back to Abe's place. They picked up their six-shooters and headed back to Morristown to have it out with Hart and Uhrig. Sometime after the confrontation in the street, Hart and Uhrig had driven off in Hart's car headed toward Lemmon leaving dust behind.

Abe had always liked to drive fast, and when his Ford jumped the grade on Highway 12 about a mile east of Keldron, it crashed into a telegraph pole, striking it eight feet above grade. Near to flying as I can imagine. The impact completely demolished the car, so it was difficult to learn exactly what had happened. Rain had fallen by the time they were found, so the tire tracks were messed up, but it looked like more than one car had skidded off the road, and one got back on. Abe died instantly, but Tom Kane survived for a while. When they pulled Kane out of the car, he was mumbling something about being chased, Abe driving too fast, and something that sounded like gunshots. But he died before anyone could make out what he was trying to say. Abe's body and head were so badly crushed it was hard to know that it was him. The county sheriff, when he finally came on the scene, at first said he thought there was a suspicious hole in the front tire, but it was too torn up to be sure. It would have taken a high-powered rifle and a crack shot to hit that tire. The car was just too smashed up to tell, and no shell casing was reported found. No one ever found out anything about that second set of tracks, but it sure looked like someone else liked to drive as fast as Abe did. At any rate, the crash was passed off as an accident, and nothing more was ever said.

I worked the homeplace as long as I could taking care of Dad and Jim's cattle as well as my own, but when Jim got out of jail, Mother wanted him to run the place. She thought he would do better with a new start. It was time for me to move on. I had spotted a half section of land for sale some thirty miles west of Fort Yates and northeast of Thunder Hawk round about fifty miles, along with some extra Indian lands that could be leased for grazing. The land had a wet creek running through the middle with plenty of trees for protection from winter storms for the cattle. I counted up my savings and concluded I was ready to give ranching a go on my own. I was tired of being on the outside of the law or at least a little past the gray edge of the law long enough, and I had pretty much given up running booze after that last Deadwood run. Tubby had gone to raising wheat and flax—the pigs didn't pay all that well—so we had just left the still boarded up in the well, where I guess it still is. He said that Prohibition had worn out its welcome and it wouldn't last much longer anyway.

Betty had been working on that part of my life, and she insisted that I give up moonshine runs or anything else that was remotely close to the cloudy side of the law. We had been seeing a lot of each other, and I really wanted to try to please her. She said she'd marry me if I agreed to give up on all my wild ways. I made the promise, and we tied the knot. We settled into our new life on our newly purchased ranch south of Shields, North Dakota, and began to raise cattle and kids and live happily ever after. I did keep the Model T truck and couple of the double-barrels, but just for hauling supplies.

Epilogue

Bob and Betty ranched all their lives, raising nine children, to some success. Bob lived up to his promise of no more activities beyond the law, but they never got rich. They worked hard and had a full life. Bob died on the ranch in 1965 while working on a car that fell and crushed him. Betty lived to see her great-grandchildren and died of natural causes in l981.

Nobody quite figured out that the man calling himself "Two-Gun Hart" was born in Naples, Italy, as James Vincenzo Capone, the oldest of the seven Capone brothers, until an enterprising newspaper reporter discovered the truth in the 1940s. After rushing to the defense of his younger brother Alphonse in a fight with a rival street gang, sixteen-year-old Vincenzo fled New York City and eventually settled in Nebraska using the name and wearing the cowboy duds of his movie idol, William S. Hart. He had a controversial and dangerous career as a Prohibition agent and lawman on several Indian reservations throughout the West. He died in Homer, Nebraska, in 1951.

About the Authors

George Gilland has been raising award-winning cattle on his land at the Standing Rock reservation for thirty years. Gilland is a proud member of the Standing Rock Sioux Tribe. He has been president of the Lakota Ranchers Association and treasurer of the American Indian Livestock Association. In addition to ranching and farming, Gilland writes a column called "Wait a Minute, I Tell You Something" for the *Dakota Herald*.

Sharon Daggett Rasmussen loved stories about her grandmother's and mother's pasts on the Standing Rock reservation. Although she moved to Oregon when she was young, she never forgot her past connection to the land.

Rasmussen has worked in communications for several government agencies and nonprofit organizations in Washington, DC, for more than thirty years.

Both Gilland and Rasmussen are members of the Western Writers of America. Their writing has been supported by a grant from the Standing Rock Sioux Tribe.